The Oxley Crossing Romances

Book 5

Australian Rural Romance

Redeeming Josh Marten

LENA WEST

Gymea Publishing

Published by Gymea Publishing

Copyright © 2017 Lena West and Gymea Publishing.

https://www.facebook.com/LenaWestAuthor/

www.lenawestauthor.com

ISBN-13: 978-0-6482671-2-6

Lena West

Disclaimer

This story is a work of fiction.

Names, characters, places and incidents are the product of the author's imagination and are used fictitiously. Any resemblance to events, locales or actual persons, living or dead, is entirely coincidental.

Some actual locations, persons and events may be referenced in passing.

Author's Note

Nowadays members of Volunteer Bushfire Brigades receive callouts via their phones, but before mobile phones, a siren sounded at the fire station. I have taken the liberty of using both methods in this book.

Table of Contents

REDEEMING JOSH MARTEN

Dedication

This novel is dedicated to the best ever bunch of grandkids.
I love you to bits, and I'm just so proud of all of you.

1

Thea Benson ran her hands through her hair and took a quick turn around her tiny lounge room to stand, hands on hips, glaring down at the report lying on the coffee table.

"Huh!"

She flung herself back onto the settee, leaned forward and picked up the mug of rapidly cooling Russian Caravan tea. Just as well today was a late start, since this bombshell had arrived by courier before she'd finished breakfast. She had no idea how she'd ever be able to concentrate on work.

With her other hand, she picked up the report she was finding so unexpectedly troubling. If she'd ever stopped to think the matter through, which she never had, she would have expected to be over the moon at this successful outcome.

Instead, she discovered this wasn't the end at all. It was the beginning of a whole barrage of new considerations. Worrying considerations. Becoming aware of a headache brewing, she rubbed her temples.

Talk about cans of worms. What to do?

She could pick up the phone and call the number Alexis Jones, the investigator, had listed and say … What?

How should she introduce herself?

"Guess what? I'm …" she tried the words on for size only to find they didn't fit at all well. What if her call instigated catastrophic results for the recipient?

And what if she rejects me outright? Simply hangs up on me? Thea cringed inwardly. *How will I handle that?*

This wasn't some feel-good television show where a happy outcome was assured. This possibility had occurred to her before, to be hastily brushed aside as irrelevant since there had been nothing she could do until Alexis Jones completed her investigation.

But now the search was completed. Successfully. And she was faced with deciding how to use the information. Or if …

Any action of hers was going to impact not only on herself, which could be bad enough, but also on the person who was the unknowing subject of her curiosity.

I have the right to know, she insisted.

She did. But at the same time, that other person had an equal right to privacy. A person whose reaction to a face-to-face confrontation she had no way of gauging.

For God's sake. Having no idea how I feel, I'm certainly in no position to make assumptions about other people and their feelings.

All I've got is a name. Just a name. No why.

And the 'why', she suddenly realised was what was at the heart of her burning need to know.

The 'why' even more than the 'who', which she'd now been given.

But what if finding my answers ruins someone else's life? Can I live with knowing I've caused harm to others, however unwittingly? Even though they're anonymous strangers?

But they won't be strangers then.

She jumped to her feet, pacing while she considered her options. *I'll have met them by then, and they'll be real to me.*

Draining her now unpleasantly cold mug of tea, she tossed the report down again. She was achieving nothing, just circling the same questions over and over in her mind, and it was time to go to work.

One thing though, she told herself, *I know I won't just go blundering in. Somehow, I have to be certain I won't be causing harm before I act on what I've just learned.*

By the time she parked outside the shopping mall where 'Hair Today' was located, she'd decided on her initial course of action.

~~~~~

Arms akimbo, Josh Marten surveyed the property with a critical eye.

The Old Murchison Place, the estate agent had called it. It was pretty rundown, but these old places were built to last, and, raised in a family of builders, he had acquired the necessary skills to restore it to its former glory.

His eyes glowed as he envisioned the place when he'd finished with it. However, it wasn't just the house he was interested in. The house was the least of the property's attractions.

Close to the essential amenities, but far enough off the beaten track to guarantee his privacy, this property offered a large, cleared, level space to build his workshop.

And when it came to his workshop, Josh knew precisely what he wanted. A humungous shed, with tons of storage space and room to work on even the biggest commissioned pieces.

Just yesterday, after beginning what he was assured would be successful negotiations for this place, he had signed the contract for a shed which met all his stringent requirements. When he gave them the go-ahead, 'Dinkie-di Aussie Sheds' would have it up on his block in a matter of days.

There were so many new ideas crowding into his mind. He needed to get back to work.

Soon as.

Before his brain exploded.

It had taken a long time to reach the point where he could make a living from his sculptures, but after winning that competition, he'd kicked his day job in his Dad's building company last month, and could now call himself a professional artist. A full-time sculptor.

He turned to share his joy with Ellie, and his face fell, darkness descending.

There was no Ellie. And it was his own damned fault. A man was supposed to protect his woman.

It took a long moment to get his emotions under control, but by then his euphoric mood had evaporated.

Grimly, he glanced up at the neglected farmhouse. The old girl sure needed a makeover. He'd be living in his old caravan for quite a while still, he guessed, but it had been home for so long already, a few more months would be no particular hardship.

Trying vainly to rekindle his earlier enthusiasm, he picked up his toolbox and a notepad and warily picked his way through the waist-high weeds, town-bred eyes open for snakes. He made a mental note to have the yard slashed before he set foot inside the gate again. Meanwhile, he'd go over the house with a fine-toothed comb before he made his offer, and maybe he could chisel a bit off the asking price. Money was going to be tight for the foreseeable future and every saving counted.

~~~~~

Thea cruised slowly towards the bridge leading into the small country town. She noticed an attractive metal sculpture of a farmer, his dogs and sheep atop a stone wall bearing the sign, 'Welcome to Oxley Crossing'. An outlying cottage housed the local hairdresser's salon, *Hair @ The Crossing*.

Herself a hairdresser, Stylist, she grinned, correcting herself, she automatically registered such facts.

The salon's neat, prosperous appearance inclined her to look favourably on the rest of the town, but she'd see. Her holiday had barely begun, so there was no rush. Plenty of time to look around. Meet people.

One person in particular?

A frown flitted across her face. She still wasn't sure she was doing the right thing, only she had had to do *something*. She couldn't not act on the information Alexis Jones had unearthed. She simply couldn't. She'd drive herself mad.

I'll feel my way, she consoled her conscience. *One very careful step at a time. For now, it's enough to drive around and get my bearings.*

Her wheels rumbled across the timber bridge. Past the hotel, an historic iron-lace fronted building labelled *The Victoria Inn*. Nice. She'd gone online to book a room there last week before heading north on her touring holiday-with-a-purpose.

Her heart beat a little faster on noticing the newsagents next door. *Later,* she promised herself, cold feet tiptoeing up her spine. Unthinking, she had begun turning in and abruptly corrected her steering.

I'll check it out later.

On down Bridge Street she drove, confident from her studies of the town website she'd soon arrive at the service station and garage. Her faithful little Honda was gasping for a refill.

And so am I.

Her tummy gave a gentle reminder at the sight of the cheerful little café in the service centre. Breakfast was a distant memory; and dinner a future dream. If the menu didn't stand up to scrutiny she'd go back to the bakery on the corner.

An older lady wearing attention-grabbing purple glasses with an unsubtle touch of bling, obviously a local, since Thea's own car was the only one out front, was sitting alone at one of the larger tables.

Thea chose a nearby table, close enough to strike up a conversation if an opportunity presented itself. This lady had the look, unmistakeable to an experienced hairdresser, of a person who knew everything going on, and loved to chat. Before she could strike up a conversation, however, a younger woman, baby on her hip, came in.

"Hi Eddie. Take Chloe a minute, will you?" Plonking the baby in the older woman's arms, she fetched a high-chair over, placing it between them. "Hi Dad," she called, waving to the man who'd just turned Thea's burger on the grill.

"Jon! Look Chloe. Daddy's here."

This last greeting was to the young man who'd walked through the back door from the adjoining garage. The loving smile he bestowed in reply made Thea's insides melt, just watching. Enviously.

If only some decent bloke would look at me that way.

Unfortunately, no such man had yet appeared over her horizon. Feeling she was intruding by taking such overt interest, Thea turned her attention to the burger and chips the waitress slid in front of her.

Food consumed, she was about to drain her cup when a chance word from the next table caught her ear. She set her cup down again, listening hard to catch every word.

"I was talking to Dot earlier," said the older woman whom the others had called Eddie. "She said Sophie will be home this weekend. Parliament's still sitting, so Bob can't get away, but their house is ready for delivery on Monday. Sophie will be here to supervise."

Although Thea listened closely, there was no more to be gleaned, so, with no excuse not to leave, she picked up her bag. Glancing up, she found herself locking eyes with a man leaning negligently against the counter.

Deep, intense brown eyes were trained unwaveringly upon her. Eyes so dark they were almost black. Drilling deep into her very soul.

Or at least that's what it feels like, she told herself, trying to shake of the uncomfortably disturbing sensation.

Maybe it was no more than her own guilty conscience, but Thea felt the owner of those eyes was reading her mind.

Defiantly, she tilted her chin, slowly taking in the rest of him. Long, coffee-dark wavy hair tied back carelessly with a leather thong. Bushy, unkempt beard, a shade darker. Stained, well-worn work clothes sporting numerous scorch marks and an old, fraying three-cornered tear on the shirt sleeve. Blundstone boots that had never been introduced to polish in living memory. It all added up to one very scruffily dressed workman.

Someone she'd normally never accord a second glance, regardless of his impertinent stare.

Except … Those eyes.

They drew her in, more deeply the longer she looked.

Then something stirred in her memory banks. She strived to recall the memory but couldn't pin it down.

I can't possibly know him. Can I?

With a conscious effort Thea dragged her eyes away and headed for the door.

His relentless stare bored into her back, every step of the way.

It took even more effort not to turn her head for a second look.

Time to check in at the hotel.

It wasn't running away. She was merely taking the time to do a little on-site strategizing. The precious days of her holiday weren't going to be wasted. No matter how interesting the distractions which sought to divert her from her purpose.

~~~~~

Having a few errands in town, Josh had walked across the bridge, then decided to have a burger for lunch. It'd save him cooking for himself later on. He entered Mike's café in his usual quiet, unobtrusive manner, placed his order, then leaned against the counter casually observing his fellow customers.

People watching.

Some of his best ideas came from such casual encounters.

Eddie Patterson! Damn! He swore under his breath. *My own fault. Should have looked first.*

Eddie Patterson was a decent person. Unfortunately, she was also vitally interested in everyone who crossed her trail, and highly skilled at winkling out their secrets. She'd been targeting him since his arrival in The Crossing, but Josh wanted none of her neighbourly attentions. He kept himself to himself; and had no intention of getting involved in the local community, no matter how friendly everyone in Oxley Crossing appeared. He shifted slightly to avoid making eye-contact with her.

And found himself looking at a stranger.

A very attractive stranger.

A woman about Ellie's age, she had one of those short, tousled hairstyles that looked artfully dishevelled. Very stylishly tinted black with frosted tips.

But it wasn't her hair that grabbed him in the gut. It was her face. He knew he'd never seen her before, he'd remember *her* if he had. Yet he knew that face. Not well, but he'd seen it recently. The same but different, if that made sense. Faces were part of his stock in trade as an artist, and he itched to record hers.

Not the usual metal. Too hard and cold. He'd swear she was anything but. *Wood. That's the medium for her. One of those weathered ironbark chunks I picked up off the side of the road the other week. A woodlands dryad for the garden.*

He could see her taking shape in his mind, and stared unblinkingly, committing her features to memory. Lucky for him she had sat so still and quiet for so long.

Then she looked up. Looked him in the eye, and he couldn't have torn his gaze away if his life had depended on it.

Josh narrowed his eyes slightly; and adjusted his mental image.

Inexplicably, he'd assumed her eyes were dark. Chocolatey brown maybe.

Instead, they were the dark, rich colour of hive-aged wild honey. The eyes of a tigress. No tame little woodland fairy, this one. She was a warrior with a spine of steel; which he'd make sure showed in his finished work.

Just look at the way she's staring me down, he thought, excitement growing.

The mystery woman swung on her heel and pushed the door open. He tracked her through it until he lost sight of her round the corner of the building. A few moments later she drove the smart little red Honda Jazz he'd noticed outside into the street and away.

No longer held in thrall, Josh relaxed, letting his creative mind build on the image he'd envisaged. It wasn't till he was on the way out himself that the oddity of his stranger's behaviour sprang into his mind.

She wasn't just sitting quietly. She was eavesdropping on Eddie Patterson's family, he realised. *I wonder why?*

Try as he might, Josh could think of no reason anyone, least of all a stranger passing through, would find family chatter so totally riveting she would be oblivious to everything going on around her. It annoyed him that the two curious questions continued nagging away in his mind, coming between him and his urge to create.

Where do I know her face from?

Why was she eavesdropping?

2

I can't wait a minute longer. I've driven past without stopping. Twice. I've checked into the hotel. And that wasn't the quick, simple process it might sound. Thea grimaced slightly.

Now she was alone in her room, she could admit how unfair her impatience with the hotel manager Marge Morris, co-owner with her husband, Phil, had been. Under other circumstances she'd have enjoyed the woman's enthusiastic promotion of what admittedly appeared to be a pleasant country town. She sincerely hoped she hadn't betrayed her feelings. It wasn't Marge's fault she was on a mission of her own and couldn't wait to take the next step.

In spite of her desperate desire for action, Thea manufactured a whole slew of urgent tasks which had to be completed before she could leave the safety of her room. She cleaned her teeth. Brushed hair which was in no need of attention. Touched up her make-up. Changed her shoes from the sneakers she wore while driving for a pair of latest season's strappy, flat sandals. When she began lifting her carefully folded clothes from the case, she forced herself to take stock.

I'm scared

It shocked the socks off her to have to admit that demeaning truth.

After all the years of waiting; of not knowing; now the time has come, I'm so scared I'm dithering about.

Stalling.

Resolutely turning her back on the suitcase lying open on the rack, she snatched up her bag and stepped out smartly before she could change her mind.

Unpacking could wait! Her mission couldn't.

Tiptoeing down the main staircase so as not to invite another delaying conversation with Marge, or anyone else, she let herself out onto the footpath. Glancing quickly up and down the street, she turned slowly to the right. Towards the newsagents shop next door. Towards her target.

Shoulders back. Head up, she instructed herself.

No-one knows who I am. No-one's going to spring out and denounce me. Even she doesn't know I'm here. Thea breathed deeply, covering the ground quickly. *And I'm not going to tell; so what am I so afraid of?*

Continuing to tell herself there was nothing at all to fear, nothing at all, Thea pushed open the flyscreen and stepped into the newsagents, pausing one step inside to slide the screen closed again and survey the broad, open room.

An older woman with long blonde hair in a plait hanging half-way down her back stood behind the counter, tidying the display while chatting to someone out of sight in a back room.

Is she …? No.

Alexis Jones had provided a photo, and this woman wasn't the one.

~~~~~

The bell tinkled softly as someone slid the screen door open. In the back corner of the newsagents, Josh Marten looked up from the selection of art supplies Dot stocked for the schoolkids. The sketch pads weren't high enough quality for finished work, but plenty good enough to make rough drafts of his ideas, and he believed in buying local where he could.

Her again.

Opening the pad in his hand, he picked up a 4B pencil from the shelf beside him and began sketching. Working lightning fast, he managed to get several different angles of the mystery woman's face committed to paper before her expression changed, reawakening his curiosity.

~~~~~

Unobtrusively, Thea edged closer, listening intently to the conversation. The more she gleaned about her quarry, the easier it would be to calculate her next move. She picked up a book of sudoku puzzles and inched a little closer, overtly feigning interest in a rack of postcards. Taking her time making her selection.

"…and so I told him, you can be sure," the blonde said. "Anyway Luv, enough about him. I'll bet you're looking forward to seeing your Sophie again, Dot. I was that sorry I missed her wedding and all, what with being in England at the time."

So. It's Dorothy James in the back room, then.

Thea's heart quickened its beat, her hands stilling their aimless rifling through the rack of postcards.

"I wonder if marriage will have changed our Sophie much," Blondie speculated.

"Not too much, as far as I can tell, talking to her on Skype."

The hairs rose on the back of Thea's neck, hearing the soft, gentle voice for the first time.

She'd given up all pretence of looking at cards. Standing with her back to the speakers, she hung intently on their every word. Hoped Dorothy James would come through to the shop so she could see as well as hear her.

Her heart pounding, Thea breathed deeply; steadying emotions which threatened to overcome her.

~~~~~

Josh halted his sketching to simply observe.

What's she getting so uptight about?

That was when he realised the woman was doing it again.

Unaccustomed anger at her effrontery bubbled up inside him. She was listening to people's conversations behind their backs. He couldn't imagine what Dot and Jean were discussing that warranted clandestine attention, and he certainly didn't want to know.

It was the principle of the thing. He couldn't abide sneaks.

He looked at the sketches he'd done.

She didn't look like a sneak, but there was no denying her actions.

~~~~~

A noise in the back corner of the shop had Thea's head swivelling to see who was there. Her breath caught in her throat, recognising the man she mentally dubbed 'The Wild Man'. The nickname was a throwback to her childhood, when her mother used to refer to such a scruffy, unkempt specimen as 'the wild man from Borneo.' Thea hadn't heard the term recently, but it had instantly sprung to mind at the sight of this man.

He was staring at her again.

Staring in silent accusation.

He can't know who I am. Why I'm here. Can he? And even if he does, what business is it of his?

Squaring her shoulders, Thea abruptly turned her back on him.

Turned to face the counter as Dorothy James walked through from the back room, instantly banishing all thoughts of the Wild Man from her mind.

Thea's eyes drank Dorothy in.

Just like the photo in her suitcase. The one Alexis Jones had included in her report. But the photo couldn't compare with the gut-punching impact of the woman in the flesh. Thea gasped, as if she had in truth been punched in the midriff. A tiny sound, but it brought the heads of both women swinging towards her.

No!

She couldn't afford to draw attention to herself. Covering her mouth and pretending to cough, Thea fought to paste an innocent, friendly smile on her face. Randomly picking out two postcards, she walked on rubbery legs over to the counter.

"Just passing through, Dear?" Dorothy inquired mildly, popping her purchases into a paper bag and handing it back across the counter along with her change.

"Yes." It came out in a croak, so Thea cleared her throat and tried again.

"I am. But Marge at the hotel has suggested I stay a few days."

"That's our Marge," chortled Blondie. "Bet she rattled off a dozen things you oughta do while you're here."

"She did." Thea smiled. Her words emerged more easily this time.

"Oxley Crossing is well worth a few days to look around." Dorothy unwittingly echoed Marge.

"Luv your hair, Ducks." Blondie changed the subject.

"Thank you."

"But I don't know ... You sorta remind me of someone."

Thea wound up the conversation and got herself out as quickly as possible without making her exit too pointed.

Josh gathered together the supplies he'd come for, including what he'd already put to use, and headed for the counter.

Shaking, Thea tottered to the corner, slumping down on a chair outside the bakery.

She'd caught a glimpse of herself and Dorothy James, side by side in the mirror behind the counter. Two women, same profile. Short sable hair naturally frosted with grey on the elder; short artificial black frosted with white ice on the younger. Thank God Blondie wasn't any more observant.

If she intended to stay for those few days, which Thea did; although when she'd actually made that decision, she didn't know; the hair had to change. Soon as.

She had an insatiable hunger to learn more about Dorothy James, with her soft, gentle eyes and sympathetic manner. One short glimpse had only served to whet her appetite for more. Her daughter Sophie, too. Sophie who was coming home on the weekend.

It would be nice if we could be friends.

Fears and wistful thoughts alike, consigned to the back of her mind, she rose to her feet.

Coffee. She needed a good strong cup of coffee to counter the lingering shakiness in her legs, and was in exactly the right place to find it.

Out on the footpath several minutes later, Josh looked both ways along the street, wondering where the woman had gone. Walking a few steps towards the corner, he spotted her sitting outside Tan's bakery-café. As he watched, she stood, catching sight of him. She stared at him, then scurried inside.

Glancing behind her, Thea noticed the Wild Man had followed her onto the street. He stood at a distance, staring at her as if he were contemplating action. What kind of action, she dreaded to think.

Shivering, she decided to have her cuppa inside, despite the pleasant afternoon.

Although Josh waited, for what he couldn't have said, she didn't return.

~~~~~

Coffee mug drained and the Wild Man long since vanished from sight, Thea set off across the bridge to make an appointment at the hairdresser's. She needed to minimise the likeness between herself and Dorothy James before someone pinned it down and started asking unwelcome questions. The simplest way was to change her colouring to something defying recognition.

She didn't see the Wild Man again, but he saw her.

Attacking his hayfield of a front lawn on his recently-acquired ride-on mower, he noticed her entering his neighbour's hair salon, emerging a few minutes later to head back across the bridge, a swing in her step. He observed her sourly. The negative vibes aroused by her suspicious behaviour were still coming between him and his need to create.

An up-to-no-good dryad would give entirely the wrong feel to the garden he intended to turn into his private refuge from the world.

3

An insouciant smile from the alien female sporting a cap of fuchsia curls and make-up to match, took Josh aback as he wandered home over the bridge the next morning toting a couple of grocery bags.

Thea couldn't help the grin, seeing she'd stunned him momentarily into non-recognition. She gave a mental air pump. The disguise worked!

He stopped to take in the sight, then realised he was looking at his mystery woman. With his eye for shape and form, he couldn't possibly mistake the slim-hipped, lithe figure of his not-so-favourite dryad, clad today in tiny denim shorts and an almost backless top. But the hair! She was barely recognisable. He pivoted on the spot, taking in the full effect of her altered appearance as she passed him with a brisk hip-swaying walk that stirred him in places he'd prefer not to be stirred.

At the last moment she flipped him a half wave with a hand he noticed was now tipped with nails as richly pink as that improbable hair.

Yesterday she had glared at him, as if she could read his mind and didn't like what she saw there. Today she smiled. He didn't trust her about-face.

It unsettled him when people changed their colours for no apparent reason.

Snorting in dour amusement at his unwitting pun, he picked up the pace, suddenly anxious to be home.

The dryad might be off the table for now, but he had plenty of other projects crying out for his attention; and if they weren't enough, there was always the money-pit, as he'd recently started calling his voraciously demanding house.

~~~~~

"Verrry pretty."

Thea, popping into the newsagents to test the efficacy of her simple disguise on Blondie, who had observed a likeness to someone as yet unidentified, was happy to come face to face with her as soon as she set foot inside the door.

"Why, thank you, ... Jean," she said, reading the woman's name-tag. Jean, not Blondie, she told herself, committing the name to memory.

"Mind you, Ducks, I thought yesterday's frosted black do was awesome. Why the change?"

"I had the black done for a very special occasion."

True.

It still gave Thea a thrill recalling the awards night where she'd been named Stylist of the Year the evening before she left on this trip.

"I wore black lace with ultra-high designer sandals, and it did look awesome. But you know, Jean, I'm on holidays and the black was beginning to feel oppressive. It was weighing me down." If this statement made her sound like an airhead, she didn't care.

"Since Marge at the hotel has persuaded me to stay on for a few days, I popped across the bridge and had Toni Molloy change it for me. Much more holiday-like, don't you think?"

She gave a little twirl on the spot, partly because the new style did feel excitingly free and easy, but more so as Jean, blinded by loose pink curls, was no longer studying her with yesterday's head-to-one-side speculative question in her eyes.

"Look Dot. What do you think?"

Thea turned to the front to see Dorothy James come through from the back room. Her heart clutched absurdly as she held her breath, waiting on the verdict. It shouldn't matter to her what Dorothy James thought of her, but it did. A slow smile spread across Dorothy's sweet face, and Thea relaxed.

"I reckon you'll have all the girls streaming across the bridge to Toni's when they see how sassy you look, Miss …?"

"Thea. Thea Benson. I'm so happy to meet you both. It's always nice getting to know the locals when you're on holiday, isn't it? I can see from the name-tags you're Jean and Dorothy. Is it all right to use Christian names?"

"Certainly, Thea, but I usually get shortened to Dot. Being called Dorothy has me looking over my shoulder to see who else is there." Dot smiled again, immediately drawn to the colourful visitor to The Crossing.

The three women chatted a while longer, then Thea bought a magazine and went up the street to the bakery to buy a picnic lunch to take on one of the drives Marge Morris had recommended.

Giddy with supressed excitement, she walked as if dancing on air, and on the drive out of town she had to set cruise control to keep her wheels on the tarmac. She wanted to fly. Loop the loop.

She settled for turning the music up loud and singing along at the top of her voice.

4

She'd had such a good day.

Dorothy…Dot, she amended, smiling to herself. *Dot likes me. I like her too. More than I'd dared expect. I wish I could tell her … But no. I don't have the right to go turning her world upside down, just because I long to be acknowledged.* All the same, Thea was floating on air as she descended the stairs to the dining room that evening.

"Oh dear, Thea," Marge, intercepting her guest at the foot of the stairs, practically wrung her hands. "I simply hate to do this, but I'm in a bit of a pickle."

Thea was rather taken aback, but with the good mood she was in, she was in an obliging frame of mind.

"How can I help, Marge?"

"It's just that today's Friday, and quite a few of the locals often come in for dinner on a Friday evening. It's become something of a tradition, which is really lovely, but tonight EVERYONE'S booked in, all at the same time, and I'm having to bring extra tables up from the storeroom."

"What's the occasion?"

"Oh, it's not really a special occasion," Marge fluttered her hands, then clutched them in front of her. "Sophie James, Sophie Whitman as she is now, wife of our new member of Parliament, is home for the first time since Bob took up his seat down in Canberra, and her friends all want to catch up with her."

All that on one breath, Thea marvelled, waiting expectantly for the punch-line.

Marge drew another full breath and delivered it.

"Now," she almost wailed, "Josh Marten's decided to turn up as well."

Josh Marten. Thea's subconscious finally threw up the memory which had been eluding her since she'd first seen her Wild Man at the garage yesterday. Of course she knew who he was. He was that sculptor she'd seen interviewed on *Breakfast With Jackie* a few months ago.

He hadn't been looking nearly so unkempt then, but she supposed he'd been polished up a bit for the cameras.

That'll teach me to make snap judgements based solely on appearances.

"What makes his presence a problem?" Thea turned a quizzical gaze on her hostess.

"Well, you see, it's going to be a dreadful squeeze, fitting so many people into my dining room. Especially when one table is reserved for you, and Josh Marten is such a loner he won't join in with the rest. He's already said so."

With her quick wits Thea intuited what was coming and swallowed the laugh that threatened to burst out.

"You wouldn't mind being a dear and sharing your table with him, would you Thea? After all, he's a famous artist. It'll be something to tell your friends when you get home, won't it?"

An errant chuckle escaped.

I was right, Thea scored a mental one-up.

"I don't mind, Marge, but what if he refuses? You said he's a loner who's already refused to join any of the locals. I'm even worse. I'm a complete stranger."

"If he wants one of my dinners he'll sit where I put him."

Marge's tart reply surprised a giggle out of Thea as she imagined the implied threat being implemented. Josh Marten slinking out of the hotel, metaphorical tail between his legs, shaggy head lowered to his chest, a Valkyrie-like Marge Morris standing arms akimbo in the doorway. It added an extra fillip to her good mood.

"Thank you, Dear. Now I'm off to the kitchen to put the finishing touches to my roast lamb."

Her problem solved to her satisfaction, Marge, not in the least a Valkyrie scurried off, leaving Thea to her fate.

Although, having had time to think, she wasn't afraid of the man as she had been at first. Especially after her mental image of him in abject defeat. She chuckled to herself again.

Besides, it had never felt as if her personal safety was under threat, anyway; or at least not very much. Her very real fear had been that he'd see through her disguise.

If he exposed her deceit, who knew what chaos might erupt. Possibly with unfortunate consequences.

For her.

If that happened, though, she'd no longer have to pussyfoot around. She could state her case; and be accepted and rejoice; or rejected and hit the road. Either way; situation resolved.

Still, she considered her chosen strategy the better option, so would step warily around him.

Smiling armour donned, Thea sashayed into the dining room, her confidence receiving an additional boost when Dot James looked up and gave her a little wave. Her heart gave a bump when she recognised the young woman seated next to Dot. Sophie. Looking exactly as she did in her photo. For a moment, Thea wrestled with the impulse to go over and manoeuvre an introduction, but discretion prevailed. She turned again towards the table for two squeezed into the bay window.

"You're at the wrong table."

Forewarned by Marge, the surly growl didn't take Thea by surprise as it otherwise would have. The best defence being offence, she launched an immediate counterattack.

"And a good evening to you, too, Mr Marten." Thea's sunny tone matched her beaming smile. "Actually, though, you got that wrong. *You* are sitting at *my* table. Marge asked me to share with you because of the crowd."

Without breaking eye contact, she flapped her hand at the rapidly filling room behind her. Anticipation building, she waited for his response.

Josh let his eyes rove insolently over the delectable female boldly confronting him.

His tiger-eyed dryad. Clad tonight in silky floral shorts, a deceptively demure high-necked white blouse and white sandals with spindly three inch heels. Hair still fuchsia curls, he noted. Probably because Toni Molloy's salon was closed, he thought with a cynical sneer, or it probably would have been purple; or green. He took his time firing his next salvo, enjoying seeing her fidget under his intense scrutiny.

"Changed your tune since yesterday, haven't you?" he finally ground out.

Thea's left brow rose, tacitly questioning his assertion.

"Scuttled out of my path both times you saw me yesterday," he muttered, barely short of a snarl. "Today you're all smiles since you found out who I am."

Oh, this was fun. Thea let her smile widen into an amused grin.

"Gotta admit, Mr Marten, the Wild Man from Borneo look is off-putting to say the least," she drawled. "Enough to make any girl in her right mind duck for cover. As for finding out who you are, I couldn't place you till Marge mentioned your name just now. Even though I've seen you in an interview on the telly." She almost fell into a justly warranted paean of praise for his work; only turning herself into a fangirl would have handed the power over to him.

Not happening.

Returning his insolent examination, she let her eyes rove, cataloguing as much of him as wasn't obscured by the table.

He didn't look much like most people's idea of a successful man. Famous artist? Maybe, she grudgingly conceded. Hair, combed but coming adrift from the leather thong meant to constrain its wildness. Clean, though unironed clothes. Shirt old enough to have already parted company with one button. A second, hanging by a precarious thread, gaped to allow a glimpse of dark chest hair.

Oddly erotic. Thea's pulse skipped a beat. She wasn't usually attracted to men with furry pelts. *Might be interesting to broaden my horizon.* Perhaps, but she instantly squelched that idea, returning to the fray. She already had more than enough on her plate without adding a man who probably wouldn't live up to her expectations. Although …

Enough!

"But no," she answered his assumption, deliberately making it the ultimate in insults. "That wasn't it. I just figured since nobody else took the slightest notice of you, you must be harmless; so, I stopped feeling jumpy around you. Anyway …," she extended a fuchsia-tipped hand, "I'm Thea Benson. Pleased to meet you, Mr Marten."

Harmless!

No more than any other man did Josh Marten relish being told by a beautiful woman that she considered him harmless. The careless challenge tempted him, but he refused to pick up the gauntlet.

Warily, he eyed the delicate hand in front of his face, as if afraid the carefully manicured nails would transform into deadly, slashing talons. He pushed himself heavily to his feet and reluctantly reached to take Thea's hand.

It required a major effort to steel himself into trusting his work-roughened paw to its dangers.

What's wrong with me? Why do I feel off balance around this woman? His discomfort irritated him on more than one level. Maybe it was something to do with being inspired to create a piece in her image, but if so, he'd never reacted in this manner before. Reasoning his uneasiness away logically didn't appear to be working. His gut still churned as if he'd eaten something bad.

Thea clasped his hand with her usual firm grip. Their hands fused together, warmth flowing up both arms from their locked palms, secretly shocking them both. And, though neither gave the slightest indication, each was surprised by how difficult it was to release the other.

Without waiting for him to seat her, Thea escaped into her chair, inserting the width of the table between them. Wishing it were wider. There had been something … intimate. Yes, definitely intimate, about the warmth of their handshake just now. It left her feeling decidedly flustered to know she wouldn't mind being even more intimate with Josh Marten. Her breath quickened when she realised what she'd just been thinking, flustering her all over again. Surely she didn't *mean* that.

First to regain the power of speech; and determined not to show how deeply his touch had affected her, Thea breathlessly fired her next shot.

"Call me Thea, Josh. I'm not into being formally correct, and," she looked him up and down once more, generating a smirk, "you don't appear to have much use for formality either."

The woman's sheer effrontery surprised a bark of laughter from Josh.

Across the room, the sound brought Eddie Patterson's head up, a considering glance directed their way.

"Pity the girl's just passing through. She got more of a response out of Josh Marten in a few minutes than the whole town in the months since he arrived here," she commented to Barbara Morgan, before turning her attention back to her own table.

"You got that right, Thea." Josh bit his lip, sobering again.

He was beginning to enjoy the girl's company. Too much. It was one thing to draw artistic inspiration from her, but he had no room in his life for personal relationships. Ellie owned his heart and soul, and he wouldn't ever want it any other way. He bolstered his resistance to Thea's charm by letting his mind return to the puzzle of her snooping and spying on his neighbours; and went on the attack.

"What were you up to yesterday? I saw you sneaking around, listening to private conversations. These are decent people here in The Crossing. They don't deserve your prying into their affairs."

It didn't take much effort to work up some righteous indignation, clawing back the ground lost by his carelessness of the previous moment.

Caught out, and how.

Tempted to go on the defensive, Thea looked him boldly in the eye and took her time answering. Searching for words to tell the truth without addressing the true spirit of his question.

"So I was," she admitted. "And so they are. We need to go back a bit, so you understand my reasons."

She fiddled with her water glass, taking a sip to moisten a mouth which had suddenly gone dry. Fingers crossed under the table, she offered up her carefully expurgated story.

"Back in the day," she was careful to be quite non-specific, "there was a … a schism within my family. My branch ended up down south. They lost contact with the other lot. My people are all dead. I've got no-one close. Didn't bother me too much till recently, when I was looking through some family documents. I started wondering if maybe the rift could be healed."

She looked up. Josh was listening intently, a frown hiding all trace of his earlier amusement.

"Go on," he prompted.

Thea nodded.

"Yes. Well. On thinking it over, I decided not to come blundering in, announcing myself to be a long-lost rellie, and probably getting the bum's rush. I'm tip-toeing. Feeling my way. If they look like people I'd enjoy getting to know, after I'm home again, I might write a letter. Test the water. But I wanted to get a good look at them first. See how the land lies."

"Who are they? Not Eddie Patterson and her mob, surely."

"Course not. I've no idea who they are. I only listened to them because a name I was interested in came into their conversation."

"But who are they? These relatives of yours?" Josh persisted, trying to pin down the elusive likeness he'd been struck by on first seeing Thea Benson. A resemblance he now believed genuinely existed. There were no Benson's in The Crossing. Not that he'd heard of. His frown deepened.

"No-one you need be concerned about." Thea waved a hand, airily dismissing the whole subject. "I've seen them from close enough, so I've no need to sneak around any longer. Besides, I'll be gone soon." She closed her mouth decisively. She'd said all she intended to on this subject. And not told a single outright lie.

Tacitly acknowledging her refusal to name names, Josh cast around in his mind for a new topic, thankful to be saved from making conversation by the arrival of their meals; two plates overflowing with Marge Morris's excellent roast lamb.

Josh dug in, and accurately interpreting his disinclination for small-talk, Thea followed suit, though more daintily.

With no conversation at her own table, Thea found herself automatically tuning in to the chatter from across the room. There it was again. A reference similar to one she'd heard the day before. Something about a house being delivered. She hadn't got it then; and she didn't get it now. Without thinking, she spoke aloud.

"How does a house get delivered? It's not as if it's a parcel being dropped off at your door. Houses need to be built. It takes months."

Josh looked up from his plate. She was up to her old trick of eavesdropping, he noted, but didn't deign to comment. This time the smirk was on his face.

"Haven't spent much time in the country, have you, Thea. Out here in the sticks they do things a bit differently."

He proceeded to instruct her on the practice of building relocatable homes.

"Suits a lot of country folk because of the savings in both time and money," he concluded. About to address himself once more to his dinner, he hesitated, then added a suggestion.

"Why don't you come over for a look on Monday? Up Murchison Lane past the hairdresser's; and you already know where *she* is." He smirked again, casting a significant glance at her fuchsia locks. "Half the town's going to be there to watch. Marge ought to be able to give you a heads-up on the time the show will be starting."

As if he considered his moment of friendly normalcy a step too far, he scowled at her again and lowered his head to his plate.

Thea made a couple more abortive attempts at restarting the conversation but failed to extract another word from him.

Rude. Just plain rude. That's what he is, she grumbled to herself.

Recognising defeat when it metaphorically slapped her in the face, she gave up on him and got on with her meal, although she continued to be aware of him. Too aware of his masculine presence for comfort.

"It was nice meeting you, Thea Benson."

Startled out of her reverie by the sound of his voice, she looked up.

Josh lay his knife and fork neatly across his plate and pushed back from the table.

By the time Thea swallowed the food in her mouth and was ready to reply, he was half-way to the door. She shrugged. Josh Marten was a difficult man indeed.

"Humph!" *No point getting ideas about him. Especially ideas involving intimacy.*

"Yes," she told the waitress who hurried to clear their empty plates. "Dessert sounds good."

She'd permit no temperamental man to cut short her enjoyment of Marge's first-class catering skills.

5

It was a quiet Saturday morning in Oxley Crossing. Hungry for another friendly encounter with her quarry, Thea popped in and out of almost all the shops the town boasted. On the hunt. Although she met a host of interesting characters she wouldn't mind knowing better, she'd obtained not one single sighting of the two people who most interested her. Not even in Dot's newsagency, where Jean and another woman, Rose, were taking care of business.

Neither did she catch so much as a fleeting glimpse of that wild man, Josh Marten. Not that she looked for him.

Not really. Except possibly to avoid him.

So she told herself, and almost believed it; denying the sneaky inner woman who thought she might relish another run-in with the prickly sculptor.

Forced to admit defeat, she bought herself another picnic lunch and headed out to Rainbow Falls. According to Marge, Morgan's Creek widened into a deep pool below the Falls. There were barbecue facilities, a playground and a sandy beach.

Sounded more fun than the municipal pool. More like the afternoons on Bondi Beach she was used to. The rising temperature raising a film of perspiration across her brow, Thea stuffed swimmers and a towel into her bag and headed on out. She was glad she did when a crowd of locals enjoying the day by the Falls invited her to join them, making up the numbers for an impromptu game of cricket after their swim.

No day was ever wasted if it brought the chance to make new friends, however fleeting. Although, that said, the beach at Rainbow Falls was nothing like Bondi. Except for people enjoying themselves getting wet, maybe.

Sunday was shaping up to be a repeat of the day before, except that on turning a corner, she caught a brief glimpse ahead of her of the James ladies leaving church. Hoping to finally wrangle an introduction to Sophie, Thea stepped up the pace. Even at a near run, she failed to come up with them before they disappeared through a dark blue front door; ushered in by one of the women they'd been with at dinner on Friday night.

Not my day.

Thea fanned her hot, sweaty face, deciding to fill in what promised to be a sweltering afternoon with another visit to Rainbow Falls. At least it would be cooler there.

Today, only a rowdy group of teenagers larking about in the water disturbed her peace as she lay on her towel under a shady tree, the latest Regency offering from Arietta Richmond her sole companion.

~~~~~

Last day.

Thea leaned closer to the mirror, carefully applying her heavier than usual make-up. Vivid. Vibrant.

And hopefully short of outright vulgar.

Especially when coupled with the avant-garde jungle print sun-suit. She cast a disparaging eye over her reflection, debating whether or not to tone her image down a notch.

Last chance.

She took out her photos of Dot and Sophie, comparing them with what she knew to be her own normal style and colouring, and shook her head.

Without the distraction of her colourful disguise, with her natural brown hair, she'd look so like the both of them Blind Freddy would notice; and guess who she was.

I'm not ready for that!

Not ready for all the hoo-ha if she was recognised, but still, Thea desperately wanted to get close; and today's number one show in town would give her the best opportunity she'd ever get.

Sophie was taking delivery of her new house; and Thea planned to be right there beside her.

Long enough at least to exchange a few words. Yearning for better acquaintance with Dorothy James, she hoped Dot would be there too.

Wondering if Sophie would be as pleasant a person as Dot, Thea gave Marge a cheerful wave and set off for Murchison Lane. As soon as she stepped outside, she realised there was no need to check her map for directions.

The thundering roar of the heavy trucks, each carrying a separate section of the house, could be heard from quite a distance as they worked their way through the gears, noisy air brakes slowing them for the turn onto the gravelled side road.

She wasn't the only one off to watch, and she fell into step with Lori, the hotel waitress whom she now knew quite well. Several others, also on foot, were headed in the same direction.

"Not much parking on Murchison Lane. It won't be appreciated if the trucks can't get in," Lori explained when Thea commented on the number of pedestrians. "This is so exciting, Thea," she enthused. "One day there's just an empty paddock, and the next there's a brand new house sitting there. My boyfriend and I reckon this is what we'll do when we get married. Of course, that's a bit down the track still, but we're making plans."

Replying suitably, Thea envied Lori her confidence in the future.

Lucky Lori. She silently prayed the girl's trust would be rewarded.

She herself had never experienced the kind of relationship which led to planning a shared future. Her boyfriends had all seemed so promising in the beginning. Then they showed their true colours. Dropkicks and losers the lot of them. Thinking a girl who liked a bit of fun was a brainless twit who could be used however they pleased, then dropped when a better prospect caught their eyes, or she refused to come across. The ones who insulted her by offering cheap baubles as payment for their pleasures were the worst; treating her as if she was some sort of amateur prossie.

These days she could pick them a mile off, but it hadn't always been that way. She'd been burned more than once, and had now pretty much given up even the trial first dates, preferring the reliable company of her girlfriends.

It was all enough to turn a girl off romance forever.

Maybe I ought to move to Oxley Crossing.

The thought flashing across her mind took Thea by surprise until she considered it. The listening and watching Josh Marten had objected to had gleaned her a far broader local knowledge than she'd been seeking, and in the few days she'd been here she had observed more truly loving relationships than she had in all her years in Bondi.

Appealing as it felt, moving here had only been a casual thought. One she promptly dismissed out of hand, but the reminder that there were still a few decent blokes around cheered her up.

Is Josh Marten one of them?

With the huge log on his shoulder weighing him down, he didn't look too promising at first sight.

Pity I won't be around long enough for second, and even third, sights.

Lori doing most of the talking while Thea wallowed in morose introspection, they maintained a desultory conversation as they walked the short distance to the building site.

Abrupt silence, almost an assault to the ears, reigned, as the drivers of the house-laden behemoths switched off their ignitions in near unison.

41

A half-hearted chortle from a kookaburra followed up by a family of magpies' more assertive carolling brought a smile to Thea's face which widened into a cheerful grin as a flock of galahs, their pink rivalling her own, swooped down to roost along the ridge pole of a section of truck-bound house, adding their raucous call to the sounds of Nature reclaiming Her territory.

Brilliant sunshine broke through the thin cloud cover which, all morning, had given the heartbreaking illusion of imminent crop-boosting rain. The rays bestowed their blessing on the flat paddock where Sophie Whitman hurried forward to confer with a gang of hi-vis jacketed workmen.

At her side lumbered the man Thea knew from revisiting the Oxley Crossing website to be Bill Whitman – shire president; proprietor of *Oxley Crossing Meats*; father of Robert Whitman, MHR, and, last, but not least, Sophie's father-in-law. Also, according to that very informative guide to life in The Crossing, his wife, Hazel Whitman, CWA treasurer, was the woman hanging back from the conferring group along with Dot James.

Thea gave the phone in her bag a surreptitious pat. Wonderful little machine. Such a fount of knowledge; wherever and whenever. Letting her desires guide her feet, she took an involuntary step in Dot's direction.

"Over there, Thea." Lori caught her arm, pointing to a tree-topped knoll across the road. "We'll only be in the way down here. Better view from up there, and a bit of shade as well, now the sun's come out."

Thea gazed wistfully over her shoulder for a moment, then dutifully followed her guide.

Lori, born and bred on a farm, had already clambered through the fence. Laughing at Thea's ineptitude, she held the strands of barbed wire apart for Thea to scramble through without getting hooked.

"Need some practice at this if you intend to spend much time out in the sticks. Watch your feet!"

"Ugh."

Thea performed a quick shuffle to avoid stepping in a cow-pat. Nervously, she looked around the paddock to locate its creator. "You forgot to mention we'd be sharing with a herd of cattle, Lori."

"Not scared, are you?"

"Not many cows in Bondi," Thea prevaricated.

Lori cracked up at Thea's dry comment. She opened her mouth to tease but thought better of it. Thea had been really nice to her, showing her how to better manage her unruly blonde hair, and giving her a few tips on make-up and fashion.

Her boyfriend had been suitably appreciative, which, to Lori's mind, made the extra effort worthwhile.

"Cows are big," she said, smiling sympathetically, "but most of them are really gentle. No need to worry today, though, Ted Lanner reckoned people might want to sit up here, so he moved the herd over to the next paddock."

Sure enough, there were quite a number of spectators with the same idea as Lori.

"Over here, girls. You can share my blanket."

"Why aren't you at work, Joey Lambert?"

Joey pulled Thea down on one side of him, shuffling over to make room for Lori on his other side.

"Afternoon shift." Dismissing Lori with his succinct reply, Joey turned to Thea. "Can't tear yourself away from me, Thea?" he winked, and held large, capable hands to his heart.

She laughed, understanding perfectly that she didn't make his heart beat the slightest bit faster any more than hers did for him, in spite of the melodramatic clowning.

Joey had been the one to invite her to join his team at the Saturday cricket game at Rainbow Falls. He'd flirted outrageously, and they'd had fun, both fully aware it was going nowhere. She suspected he had more depth of character than was immediately apparent. Probably more than even he was aware of. He'd make a good friend.

Pity I won't be around after today.

"Hey Sophie!"

At Lori's shout, Thea looked up. The conference with the workmen concluded, Sophie, her mother and in-laws were making their way up the knoll to sit in the shade. Not that there was much unoccupied shade left. The older trio set up their folding chairs in a narrow gap behind Joey's blanket, while Sophie unrolled a beach towel alongside Thea.

"You must be Thea Benson," she said, smiling, her hand out-thrust in the universal gesture of friendship. "Sophie Whitman. I've been hearing about the pretty girl with pink hair. I like it."

This time Thea's heart did accelerate its beat. Sitting shoulder to shoulder with Sophie, she felt almost too choked up to speak.

This was better than anything she'd hoped for, especially since she'd almost accepted this meeting wasn't going to happen.

"It's a bit high-maintenance, but fun," she croaked out, cursing herself for the blank mind which reduced her to uttering such inanities. On such an auspicious occasion, why couldn't she come up with something more profound? Something memorable?

"Hello Thea." Dot leaned forward, placing her hand lightly on Thea's shoulder to attract her attention. "Let me introduce you to Hazel and Bill Whitman. Their son is married to my Sophie who's sitting beside you there."

Thea turned to greet the Whitmans, exchanging a few friendly comments with them, basking in Dot's approval of her.

If only ...

But she'd been given so much more than she'd expected when she arrived in The Crossing. It would be greedy to ask for more. Thea decided to make the most of this heaven-sent opportunity. Speaking hypothetically, she'd told Josh Marten on Friday night she might write a letter, but having assessed the situation, she didn't think so. She'd heard not a single whisper to suggest her news would be welcomed; and having met Dot and Sophie, she couldn't bear the thought of being rejected by them. She would have to be content with the handful of treasured memories she'd gleaned on this short visit to Oxley Crossing.

The lead truck roared into life. The audience turned as one, following its progress as the driver, guided by the foreman's hand signals, skilfully lined his load up with the markers.

He'd done this a time or two before, making no mistakes. Correctly positioned in next to no time, the house section was jacked up, and the truck pulled smoothly out from beneath it to cheers from the knoll.

It was quite late in the day before all the trucks had been unloaded. There was still a lot of work to be done before the house would be liveable, but what had been achieved in one day seemed incredible to Thea. Both Lori and Joey having left for work, and Sophie and her family conferring with the foreman again, Thea started back into town on her own.

~~~~~

At first glance, Josh had thought the flash of pink over on the knoll where the townies were getting a grandstand view was some woman's hat. But the colour niggled at him, urging him to taking a closer look.

Thea Benson! Looks like a bloody galah with that pink mop, he scoffed, trying to work up a healthy disdain for the life model of the dryad already peeping out from the iron-bark stump sitting in the shade alongside his ratty old caravan.

Well that settled that. He'd been half inclined to amble across and watch from the fringes of the mob, but no way was he letting himself get drawn into the orbit of that pink-haired witch. Thoughts of her had ruined his sleep since Friday night, something which went very much against his grain. He had no right to notice a woman. Any woman.

Once, he'd had the comfort and inexpressible joy of a woman in his life. It was his own fault she was no longer with him. Because of the way he'd failed her, he didn't deserve a second chance in that department.

All he could do now, was dedicate his talent and his miserable, worthless life to Ellie and hope she would forgive him in his next life. If there was a next life. If there wasn't, he had no hope at all.

He skulked in the back of his shed, working on a piece destined to grace the foyer of a new casino being built at Barangaroo.

Fighting the lure of pink curls and gurgling, infectious laughter. Afraid he'd get no peace until the damned woman went back where she came from.

~~~~~

As Thea passed Sophie's next-door neighbour on Murchison Lane, she wondered who owned the old house. Camouflaged by scaffolding, it still looked as if it would be something special when its restoration was completed.

The sort of house she'd once dreamed of living in. A dream populated by a loving husband and several mischievous kids. A dream long since consigned to the land of might-have-beens. She sighed, not entirely reconciled to the loss of her dream future.

Bright light flared from the depths of the huge shed alongside the house where someone was welding.

Someone too busy to come out and watch today's show, Thea observed idly, admiring the unseen workman's adherence to duty.

She'd seen the flashes off and on all day, but her one glimpse of the industrious welder had been of a man in an even more complete disguise than her own.

Overalls, heavy welding gloves and a helmet with faceshield lowered, effectively rendered him unrecognisable.

Spotting Toni Molloy in the doorway of her salon, Thea gave her a friendly wave.

"Thea Benson!" Toni called out. "This is a bit of luck. I was about to call Marge and leave a message for you to get back to me. Now I won't have to share my private business with The Crossing grapevine. Have you got time to come in?"

"Sure, Toni." Thea wondered … She and Toni had had an interesting conversation while she'd been getting her hair done. Toni had promised to keep her ear to the ground when Thea claimed she was interested in setting up shop for herself. Maybe she'd heard of something. What had only been idle talk then, suddenly bloomed into an attractive option.

Another 'What if …' idea.

6

Since Toni Molloy put a notice in the local paper announcing a change of management at the salon, Oxley Crossing had been buzzing with speculation. Everyone understood Toni's decision to retire and move to the coast to be closer to her family.

What was harder to accept was her coy refusal to say anything at all about her replacement. Except that it was someone she was absolutely positive they'd all adore. This snub was Toni's not-so-subtle payback for the time she herself had been subjected to unpleasant speculation and innuendo when her gentleman caller had ceased calling. She'd had a good life in Oxley Crossing, but even here gossip carried a nasty sting. Ever since, she'd kept her private business under her hat.

There were a few in The Crossing who had a glimmer of sympathy with her hugging the facts to herself instead of feeding them to the grapevine. Those who also enjoyed challenging the local purveyors of information. The gossips, as the unkind termed them. As a result, the stories doing the rounds ranged wildly across the spectrum; each one wide of the mark.

Loner though he was, Josh Marten had heard a great many of these fabulous conjectures, dismissing most out of hand. In truth, he was as ignorant of the facts as all the others, although, as Toni's nearest neighbour, it was assumed he would have insider knowledge denied to the rest of them. His refusal to play the game resulted in more than one disgruntled inquisitor.

"Come on Mate," Pete Hackett had cajoled when Josh had gone to the hardware store for welding supplies. "You must have seen who came to look the place over. No-one with an ounce of common sense would have bought it unseen off the internet. Or wherever else Old Toni advertised. She certainly didn't sell it through my agency." Pete, for whom real estate provided a lucrative sideline to his hardware business, was rather miffed at being done out of what he considered his rightful commission.

When appealed to, Edith Patterson, doyenne of Crossing society, had pursed her lips and shaken her head, pretending to be as baffled as her friends. What she didn't share, was her conviction that Toni hadn't advertised her business for sale at all. Eddie had combed the internet, drawing a complete blank, leading her to conclude the sale had been private. A friend of a friend, maybe. Or ...

Without confirmation, the idea forming in Eddie's head was one she kept to herself. Her reputation for knowing what was going on before anyone else having been built as much on knowing when to hold her tongue as it was on her exhaustive knowledge of local affairs, it wouldn't do to stick her neck out and be proved wrong.

Hers was the same idea slowly gaining ground in Josh Marten's head.

One he fervently hoped was wrong.

He'd cursed Thea Benson more than once during the past weeks. His memory of her continued to stir physical reactions in him which he really didn't want to feel.

That part of his life was long over, all his passion now channelled into his work.

Except that every time he picked up his chisels and faced his half-completed dryad, it was to discover his creativity was blocked. Thank God it was only the dryad which was affected. He'd made no progress on her at all.

The dryad in Thea Benson's image.

God, I hope Toni's mystery buyer isn't her.

He continued to hope and pray right up until fate laughed in his face.

On moving day, he lent a hand-truck to Toni's sons, and was helping them load their mother's furniture, along with half a lifetime's accumulation of bits and pieces she couldn't bear to part with, into their hired Pantech.

The doors slammed on the last overloaded box. Josh straightened, hands supporting his lower back, stretching the kinks out. With a hiss, he sucked back a curse he'd prefer not to give voice to in front of a woman.

A little red Honda, one he recalled from several weeks back, turned into the drive. Behind its wheel the driver, sporting an all-too-familiar cap of vivid, fuchsia curls, waved vigorously through the open window.

Josh's gut took a sickening nosedive.

The suspicion he'd been holding at bay ever since recalling the woman's casual mention of her profession at dinner that night, had been realised.

At the same time, his body stirred with an excitement his head strenuously denied.

"Thea! You made good time. Just pull in over there, out of the way." Toni hurried to embrace Thea as she exited the car.

Thea returned the hug, her mind racing.

Meeting Oxley Crossing's grumpy artist again was a given, but she hadn't expected it to occur so soon. Her heart had skipped a beat at the sight of his wild head topping tattered overalls. She'd had eyes for no-one else until Toni's shouted greeting brought her back to earth with a bump.

Carefully keeping her back to the man, she schooled her features into a semblance of nonchalance.

"Come and meet my sons, Eric and Harry. Of course you remember Josh from next door." Thea shook hands with Toni's burley sons, then turned to Josh.

So Josh Marten is the boy next door, is he?

Nonchalance be damned!

Her bland smile twitched into a devilish grin.

"Hi Josh. Good to see you again. I hadn't realised you'd be my boy next door."

Although there was nothing of the boy about him. Her eyes did a rapid sweep, covertly assessing his finer points. He was all man. One hundred percent.

And, judging by the annoyance he made no effort to hide, less than enthused about meeting her again. Temptation and challenge in one lean, well-muscled masculine package.

Such a pity he hides himself away behind all that hair. Thea felt a strong conviction she'd like the face hidden behind the rampant growth if ever it was revealed to view. She had nothing against well-maintained beards and long hair, but the very unkempt wildness of Josh Marten's made her fingers itch for her scissors. She wondered whether he could be persuaded to tame it.

"Come on in, everyone. I'm just putting the kettle on for lunch. Eric was about to go over the bridge and fetch some rolls. You too, Josh." Toni caught Josh by the arm, towing him along with her. Preventing his attempted escape. "You've worked like a Trojan alongside my boys. The least we can do is feed you."

Thea smothered a grin and brought up the rear as they trooped inside, deliberately choosing to sit beside Josh in the circle of folding chairs in Toni's kitchen. She was still at his side half an hour later when Toni, chairs and tea making paraphernalia stowed in the boot of her car, drove of in the wake of the truck, Harry Molloy at its wheel.

"Drive safely," Thea called, waving madly until her friend was out of sight.

"I guess the story about coming to The Crossing to suss out some long-lost relatives was a furphy? You were here to look over the salon."

It came out more of an accusation than a question. Josh had been stewing quietly over her perfidy to distract himself from the effect Thea's proximity had on his libido.

Her light floral perfume, clearly recalled from their shared dinner, had wreathed around his head all through lunch, making clear thought almost impossible.

"Though God only knows why you went through all that rigamarole of keeping it a secret you were the new owner."

"Umm?"

Startled, Thea swung to face him. Now she was the one making no bones about being annoyed. Curmudgeonly behaviour was one thing. Outright rudeness quite another. She had no intention of letting him get away with it, thereby setting a precedent for future encounters.

"Actually, Josh ..."

The touch of acid in Thea's dulcet tones made Josh uncomfortably aware of just how rude he'd sounded. He usually managed to avoid being openly confrontational, even when provoked.

Which I was, he reminded himself.

"I told you the truth about my reason for visiting The Crossing. Learning Toni wanted to sell up was a bonus. I've been planning to buy a place of my own for quite a while, and when she offered, I accepted. As for the secrecy, that was all her idea. She reckoned it'd generate extra interest and guarantee a good roll-up next week with everyone coming for a sticky-beak. The first time. Second time will be because they'll get the best haircut they've ever had."

While talking she'd been determinedly steering him towards the gate. If all he wanted to do was make her feel bad, he could get lost. This was meant to be a happy day for her.

Shutting the gate smartly behind him, she headed back inside to take possession of her business. Her own. No more bosses for Thea Benson.

From now on, *she* was the boss.

She walked around the salon, which she had bought walk in/walk out, possessively touching chairs, wash-basins, dryers. Running her fingers along the fully stocked shelves.

Walk in/walk out meant no down-time during the takeover except for today, Friday, and Saturday morning. Come Monday, she had a full appointment book, Toni had informed her over the phone, but she checked for herself anyway, gloating over her good fortune.

Forgetting about her annoying, intriguing, next-door neighbour.

For now, anyway.

Mine!

To own her own salon was a long-held dream come true. Joyful excitement flooded her being.

Feet tapping to a rhythm only she could hear, Thea spun across the room from one station to another, stopping just long enough at each to let her joy explode in bursts of the dance she'd been practicing at her last tap class. Last ever class, maybe, but it wouldn't be her last dance. No way. She danced for the love of it. The music. The euphoria of letting her body express her emotions. As now.

Facing the mirror-tiled wall which visually more than doubled the size of the modest salon, she slowed to a sensuous, steamy number.

It was so ridiculously at odds with the ultra-practical jeans, sweatshirt and boots she'd worn for arranging furniture and unpacking boxes, she laughed aloud.

Although she'd taken possession of the keys earlier in the day, the task of moving in still lay ahead of her. She was caught up in the hiatus between Toni Molloy's possessions being uplifted earlier that morning by her two hefty sons, and her own meagre goods and chattels being delivered this afternoon.

Which would be right about now.

She glimpsed the delivery van pulling up outside *Hair @ The Crossing;* and ran outside to greet the driver and his offsider.

7

Damn it all!

Throwing down the sketch pad filled with page after page of unsatisfactory drawings, Josh stalked off across the yard, not bothering to enter via the gate which was round the other side of the building. The low fence between the properties posed no obstacle. Without slowing his advance, he vaulted the inoffensive structure and marched in a belligerent beeline towards the glass-walled sunroom built onto the back of the cottage.

His usual peaceful early morning routine of coffee while designing new sculptures, or simply sketching whatever caught his eye, had been totally disrupted by that woman's music at the crack of dawn. Every morning since her arrival.

Why couldn't she listen to the birds as he did, or turn the volume down to something lower than the crack of Doom? Toni Molloy had never impinged on his untrammelled isolation. He didn't see why he should have to put up with it from Thea Bloody Benson.

Bad enough she haunted his sleep, appearing in disturbing erotic dreams that left him irritable and … hungry. Hungry for what he no longer had. Would never have again. This week had seen him reduced from a productive, albeit lonely, existence to a state of perpetual dissatisfaction, seething with unresolved anger.

He couldn't go on this way.

She … her presence, was interfering with his work. And since work was all that kept him sane and connected to the human race, he had to find a solution.

He was having it out with her. Now. This minute.

It would be wonderful if she took fright and moved out. Wonderful, but highly unlikely, considering she'd only just moved in.

Well, she'll have to learn to do things my way. Or …

His mind boggled.

It didn't improve his temper any to realise that short of complaining about the noise, there wasn't much he could do if she proved recalcitrant. It simply wasn't in his nature to harm a woman. Or any one at all, for that matter.

Fuming, he strode up to the door. All the louvered windows in the room were open to their widest, allowing the deafening music to stream through unimpeded, drowning out the competing kookaburra chorus from down by the creek. Josh raised his fist to thump on the door jamb to attract the woman's attention.

He froze on the spot, fist still raised.

Inside the sunroom, now stripped of all furnishings except for a powerful ghetto-blaster sitting under the power point in the corner, Thea danced. Leaping, stepping and twirling, pirouetting and gliding, she covered the floor in perfect synchronisation with the music, from end to end of the bare, polished timber floor and back again, oblivious to the malign presence at her door.

Josh stood spellbound, the breath caught in his throat. This was his dryad as he'd imagined her. Wild. Free. Alive. The very elements he'd lost sight of, resulting in his artistic block. A block abruptly shattered. His hands, aching for the familiar weight of his chisels, felt as if they possessed a life of their own. He stepped back, about to return and let them have their way. He'd deal with Thea and her noise another time.

A crashing finale brought the performance to an end. Thea, breathing heavily after her exertions, ran across to eject the CD from the machine.

At a movement behind her, sensed rather than seen, she spun round to face the door. The CD fell unheeded to the floor. A scream ripped from her lips. She pressed her hands against her pounding heart. Cheeks, flushed from exercise, suddenly paled; then the colour flooded back again as she recognised the man who stood in the doorway behind her.

Ears ringing in the sudden silence, so abruptly shattered by Thea's ear-piercing scream, Josh was halted in his tracks.

"Josh Marten," Thea yelled, only a few decibels lower than her scream of a moment before. "What do you think you're doing, creeping up on me like Freddy Krueger? You scared me half to death."

"Sorry. Sorry." Josh held placating hands up in front of him. Shuffling a half-step back, he hoped she realised he wasn't intending harm.

The sheer beauty of her dancing, followed by the scare he'd given her, had temporarily taken the wind out of his sails, but he could hardly race off now without explaining his presence. Looked like he'd be dealing with her today, after all. Frustration at being forced to defer what he really wanted to do rapidly rekindled his anger. Josh gathered his grievances around him like a cloak. Building up steam, he lashed out while she was still off balance.

"If you hadn't had your bloody music cranked up so loud, you'd have heard me," he bellowed, striving for dominance in the forthcoming argument he was once again spoiling for.

Stunned by his verbal attack, Thea stared at him, then looked behind her at her sound machine. Slowly, she bent to pick up the CD. Dusting it off, she carefully returned it to its case.

"Hope it's not scratched." She began walking towards the kitchen. "Oh, come on."

She waved an impatient hand, gesturing for him to follow her. When he hesitated, she elaborated.

"You must have a reason for being here. Come in and I'll put the kettle on while you tell me about it."

Eyes to the front, she kept walking.

Josh followed. It was either that or be left standing on the doorstep.

He followed mindlessly, eyes glued to the sway of the taut, feminine derriere clad in skin-tight black lycra.

Twin globes perfectly moulded to fill a man's hands.

Now the tingle in his palms wasn't generated by a need to wield tools. It took more effort than it should have to override his prurient desires. Another source of aggravation added to the preceding annoyances.

He arrived in the kitchen to see her pouring a large glass of cold water from a jug in the fridge. Sipping it, she filled the kettle, one-handed, and switched it on. Reaching into the cupboard above the workbench, she brought out two large fine-china mugs with wildflowers painted on the sides. Without asking, she measured leaves into a teapot. Glancing over her shoulder, she flapped an impatient hand at him.

"Sit down. Please. This won't take long, then we can talk."

She'd only allowed herself a quick glance at him, but she'd recognised the signs of a man consumed by rage. It was radiating from him, dousing the glow of her exercise-induced endorphins. A man in such a dangerous mood needed careful handling. While she busied her hands with tea-making, she considered how best to defuse the situation.

Josh sat.

He'd striven to regain the righteous anger that had driven him to her door, but she was making it hard. How could you have a knock-down, drag-'em-out fight while politely sipping tea?

The answer was, you couldn't. Not if you'd been raised by a mother who believed in manners. Which only fanned the flames of his rage as he sat, seething in silence, watching Thea brewing her tea.

Tea, for God's sake! At the very least a man needed coffee to deal with a woman who made him mad as a cut snake!

Thea finally slid a steaming mug across the table to him, and sat opposite, cradling her own between loosely clasped hands. She breathed in the fragrant aroma, then raised sober eyes to meet his.

"Tell me what I've done to make you so angry with me," she asked, her voice soft and low. Placating.

"You play your blasted music so loud I can't think." The words exploded from him, making her flinch.

"Josh, I'm so sorry." His earlier comment had alerted her to the nature of his complaint, and she acknowledged her fault and hastened to explain. "The dance studio I used to attend always played the music loud to drown out the noise from the gym downstairs. I didn't think. I just turned the volume up to what I was used to." She reached across to lay her hands on the one clutching his mug in a death-grip. "I wish you'd spoken up sooner, Josh. I want to be a good neighbour. I really do. I'll keep the sound turned low from now on."

"Well." He'd expected her to argue the point. Her ready acceptance of her guilt left him without a leg to stand on. Like a damp squib, his anger fizzled out. "See that you do." Abstractedly, he took a gulp of tea. And almost spat it out. "God, Thea. Don't you have any sugar? Or milk?"

Relieved the crisis was safely averted, Thea giggled.

"I'll fetch some from the salon," she said, rising from her chair. "I don't use either, but I keep some for my clients. Won't be a moment."

His tea doctored to his satisfaction, and a plate of hot, buttered toast between them, Thea got Josh talking, asking about his sculptures. Feeling guilt of his own for getting so steamed up when all he needed to do was speak to her, one reasonable adult to another, he was more forthcoming than usual. He'd even begun to settle in and enjoy her company, when she looked at the clock, jumping to her feet with a muted shriek.

"Look at the time! Josh, finish your breakfast, but I've got to hit the shower or I'll never be ready to open on time."

Abandoned to his own devices, Josh hurriedly swallowed the last mouthful of toast and was half-way to the door when he stopped, and looked back over his shoulder. The shower was already running, and he couldn't help picturing a naked, soap-slicked Thea Benson rinsing the sweat from her lithe body. It was definitely Thea, not her imaginary alter ego he envisioned, innocently taunting him; innocently tempting him. Sometimes a vivid imagination was a distinct disadvantage. He needed to get out of there. Now. Before his baser instincts got the better of him and he joined her under the shower. But still he hesitated.

Huffing a little, he surveyed the mess of crumbs and empty plates. He couldn't leave the cleaning up to Thea when she was already late due to his visit. He picked up the mugs and took them to the sink. Five minutes later, the kitchen spick and span, he set off again, eager to escape the images of Thea in her shower, which he just knew were going to haunt him for the rest of the day.

~~~~~

Bless the man.

Thea smiled.

He'd not only set the kitchen to rights, he'd even remembered to return the milk and sugar to the tiny kitchenette in the back corner of the salon. No longer needing to rush, she strolled across to the nearest mirror to critically survey her reflected image.

Nose wrinkling, she finger-teased those ridiculous pink curls. The dominant shade fought her natural colouring. And won. Without make-up she looked sallow, her eyes a murky light brown. She so wanted to return to being her natural self, only it was still too risky. But she'd be making a change to something less … less pink, she decided. That was for sure. She'd let the curls grow out, too. Back to the smooth, straight cap that threw her high cheek bones into relief. Maybe when people were fully accustomed to seeing her in various guises, they wouldn't even notice any similarities to others they knew when she reverted to being entirely herself again.

Busy as she was all day, Thea made time for one extra task during her short lunch break. Leaving Vera Nicols, the assistant she'd inherited from Toni, along with Lisa Tan, a second-year apprentice, in charge of the salon, she threw together a batch of ANZAC biscuits. She owed Josh Marten an apology for disturbing his peace; and also a thank-you for cleaning up the kitchen.

Late that afternoon, the salon sparkling and ready for the next day's influx of clients, Thea filled a plate with the biscuits and set off, taking the long way round through the front gate, to deliver them to Josh. Despite parting amicably in the morning, she was a prey to nerves. The dratted man was so unpredictable.

Would he growl at her to go away, or smile and welcome her in? She hoped the later, as she felt more drawn to him than ever.

Given the slightest encouragement, or maybe no encouragement at all, she'd like to see what might come of the attraction between them. An attraction she was sure was mutual. She'd glimpsed a quickly concealed look of hot masculine desire in Josh Marten's eyes that made her blood heat and an ache pulse deep in the core of her feminine self. It was a look she recognised because she'd seen it before, in other men who'd made no effort at all to disguise their interest. Who hadn't stirred her to half the extent Josh Marten did.

Following the sounds of gentle tapping of metal on metal, she came upon her quarry on the shady side veranda of the old house. The scaffolding was gone now, and the lovely old building gleamed with a fresh coat of white paint. The eaves and gutters were trimmed in a deep emerald green. Stumbling as her foot caught on a broken floorboard, she juggled to keep her balance – and the biscuits on the plate. The tapping stopped.

Josh had been lost, freeing his dryad's long tresses from the wooden matrix of the ironbark stump. Unconsciously he'd registered the creak of weathered veranda boards signalling a visitor. Someone heavier than the monitor lizard which had taken to paying him a curtesy call at meal times in the hope of winning a hand-out. The stumble and gasp of his visitor tripping on the broken floorboard he hadn't gotten around to replacing were loud enough to impinge on his consciousness. Sighing, he lay down the chisel and hammer and stood to meet whoever had decided to intrude on his peace and quiet.

"Afternoon Thea."

He noted she was freshly made-up and dressed in something casual and fetching. Different to the smock he usually saw her in on work days. Warily, he watched her approach. He'd spent most of the day trying unsuccessfully to expunge her image from his mind. He didn't need her here stirring him up again.

"Hi Josh. I've brought a peace offering." She held the plate out to him. "Hope you like ANZACs."

Her beguiling smile caressed, and even though a good two metres separated them, Josh felt his gut tighten and a shiver run up his spine.

"Oh. I thought you worked in metal." Abandoning the plate of biscuits on a small table already bearing several dirty coffee mugs and an assortment of small tools, Thea tip-toed forward. "May I look?"

"Not much to see yet. She's got a long way to go." Josh shrugged. Short of throwing the cover back over the stump, he couldn't very well prevent Thea from looking. Besides, he was intrigued to see her side by side with the life-sized piece she'd inspired. His eyes roved from figure to figure, comparing. Noting similarities and differences. While the dryad was boyishly slender, Thea's breasts were fuller: riper. Her hips more rounded. He tried to convince himself the urge to touch sprang from the artist, not the man, but it felt too carnal to be artistic in origin.

"That hair looks so real I can almost see individual strands. It doesn't look like wood at all. Are you going to carve her out fully from the tree?"

Thea glowed with delight that Josh allowed her to see his work.

This beautiful nude female figure with long hair swirling about her form down to mid-thigh, a short sword gripped in her right hand, intrigued her. Half turned away from the viewer, her bare flesh was almost modestly shrouded, in Lady Godiva fashion, by her hair.

She likes her.

Gruff voice hiding his pleasure, Josh edged closer.

"No. She's of the tree. One with it. She's sort of materialising from it. There's a bit more to do on her hair, still, then the face."

Hands shoved deep in his pockets where they were safe from the temptation to reach out and touch, he studied the two figures, eyes switching slowly from one to the other. Without thinking, he opened his mouth, and words he immediately wished he could retract came tumbling out.

"I don't suppose you'd like to pose for her, would you?"

8

An unexpected bonus of having Thea pose for him, since she'd naturally jumped at the chance, was that unexpectedly, Josh became more relaxed in her presence. Even began to look forward to seeing her scramble over the fence and cross his wilderness of a front yard on feet so light they appeared almost to be dancing. A beaten path now showed anyone in a position to observe it, that there was regular traffic between two of the houses on Murchison Lane.

Josh still found Thea's smile a touch too provocative for comfort. Her luscious body still exuded pure temptation; but since she never stepped over the invisible line he'd drawn between them, he relaxed.

Finely honed instincts for self-preservation warned him she'd be more than willing, if given the slightest encouragement, so, overtly remaining the taciturn grouch she knew, he was careful not to offer any. It wouldn't be fair of him to raise expectations he'd not be able to meet.

Lust after Thea Benson he might, but it was Ellie who deserved his loyalty.

Ellie who held his heart.

~~~~~

"Hi Josh. Hello Lunara." Thea greeted artist and creation. When Josh had answered her questions, explaining his dryad was more than a simple fairy; that she was a warrior protecting her forest home, the name 'Lunara' emerged from the depths of Thea's memory.

"She comes from a game a friend used to play. I liked her because she had guts. Your description sounds just like her."

Josh's only comment was a dismissive grunt, but the name had stuck. Even he used it, talking to his creation as he worked on her. Provided he was alone.

She was almost finished, and then he wouldn't need Thea's modelling services any longer. He'd miss her visits. In spite of his best intentions, she'd gotten under his skin with her damned cheerfulness. Not to mention her awakening of his darker desires. His mood lowered, his habitual grumpiness becoming more real than feigned.

He'd tell her now. No procrastinating.

Then he could get back to normal.

"I appreciate your help, Thea. However, you won't need to pose any more after today. You'll be able to go back to doing your own thing in the afternoons in future."

The lightning flash of shock that crossed her expressive face before she schooled her features to impassivity made him uncomfortable.

Damn!

He cursed silently, turning away from the pain he saw lingering at the back of her eyes. Couldn't he have phrased his announcement more tactfully? He owed her more than a curt brush-off now Lunara's face was completed.

"I'll be away for a few days," he added, trying to soften his curt dismissal.

"Oh." Thea pretended indifference to the news. If she meant no more to him than his abrupt brush-off indicated, she was glad he'd be away; or so she tried to convince herself.

I thought we were friends, and he gives me the flick. Just like that. He doesn't deserve me.

He didn't. Yet the truth hurt. She still wanted him. Craved his presence in her life.

It was a real turn-up, a man she fancied being resistant to all the lures she'd cast his way. She was more accustomed to fighting off importunate suitors than being the one doing the chasing. Unsuccessful chasing at that. Resentment smouldered.

I need to work on my technique.

"Where are you going?" She wanted to jump up and run back to the sanctuary of home, only she refused to let the damned man see she cared.

"The truck's coming tomorrow to take the piece for the casino down to Sydney. I'm going along to supervise its installation, and they want me there for the grand opening on Saturday."

"You're going to a big fancy do looking like that?" Aghast, she almost shrieked.

Looking him up and down, she sidelined her resentment for the moment. She'd got used to the wild man look, barely noticing anymore. The casino owners mightn't be so tolerant. Not when they were paying top dollar for his work.

"I've got a tux." Josh sounded surlier than ever.

"You need more than a tux if you're going to be rubbing shoulders with the toffs. We need to work on your image, Mr Famous Sculptor."

Jumping to her feet, Thea grabbed his hand. "Come on. I'll get you cleaned up and presentable."

He argued all the way across to her salon, only going along with her because he still felt guilty. He argued right up until she pushed him into a chair and flung a cape around his shoulders. He eyed Thea's fuchsia locks askance. 'Image' held bad connotations to his way of thinking. When she picked up her scissors, he made a last-ditch effort to escape whatever she had in mind.

"I like it long." Faced with Thea's inner tiger, armed with scissors, he felt a sinking trepidation.

Thea hesitated a moment, thinking over what she was about to do. It was so tempting to simply whack the lot off. All that wild hair sticking out around his head and shoulders. Thoughtfully threading her fingers through his tangled locks, she shook her head. She was bound by her own strict rules to give her clients what they wanted.

"Okay. Long it is. The beard?" Resignation tinged the question.

"Stays. I can't stand shaving. Waste of bloody time."

The afternoon had darkened into evening by the time Thea stepped back, whipping the cape away. His hair, still long enough to be tied back when he was working, brushed his shoulders. Rippling, glossy waves replaced the tangle of wild corkscrews. The beard, trimmed short and dense, lent an air of mature distinction to his face. The reflection in the mirror was that of an arresting, virile man. A sexy man on whose arm any woman would be delighted to be seen.

On whose arm Thea yearned to be seen.

Except she hadn't been invited. Her resentment smouldered anew, injecting into her voice a rarely heard tartness.

"There. My gift to the world of culture and refinement. All you need do is wash it, then run a comb through it occasionally."

"Thanks, Thea. You're a good friend. Better than I deserve."

He's got that right.

Resentment for his earlier brush-off rekindled to a blaze in Thea's breast. Now, thanks to her hard work, he'd be the target of all those predatory high-society women at the casino opening. She doubted he'd give them the cold shoulder.

Oblivious to the growing storm at his back, Josh studied his image in the mirror. The well-groomed man staring back at him was one he hadn't seen for a long time.

Too long.

Self-consciously, he realised Ellie would have been the first to tear a strip off him for letting himself degenerate into the unkempt hobo he'd become since moving to The Crossing. She'd have applauded this fresh new-look-Josh. He owed it to her to take better care of himself.

"I like what you've done for me." Embarrassed for his earlier brusque treatment of her, he tried to make amends to Thea by praising her work. Failing to raise the ready smile he'd come to expect from her, he tried harder.

"I'll take care not to revert to your Wild Man from Borneo again."

Enough was enough! Provoked beyond endurance, Thea ceased sweeping up the clippings. Carefully, she leaned the broom against the wall. Closing in behind him, she gripped his shoulders, holding him down in the chair when he made to rise.

"See that you don't, or I'll have to come after you."

Alerted to impending danger by Thea's sultry tone, he focused on her reflection in the mirror. She still wasn't smiling, but the narrow-eyed intensity of her gaze, what he'd come to think of as her tiger look, froze him in the chair.

Slowly, giving him all the time in the world to stand up and walk away, she spun him round to face her. Stepping close, her eyes locked onto his. She cupped both hands round his cheeks; and leaned closer. And closer. Till her lips tingled from the heat of his breath and, even through several layers of fabric, she felt the brush of his shirt against breasts suddenly tight and swollen.

Her pulse rate going through the roof, she feathered her lips across his. Feeling a quiver of response, she did it again, deepening the pressure. Felt it returned. Almost of its own volition, her tongue teased his lips, darting in to stroke, slow and deep, when they parted.

Josh hadn't seen it coming. She'd caught him with his guard down.

As if it was happening to someone else, Josh felt himself respond to Thea's kiss. Taking it deeper than her light caress. Her taste flooded his senses, tearing down already weakened barriers. He wanted more of her.

Needed more of her.

Taking control of the kiss, his hands rose to hold her in place. His mouth ground relentlessly against hers. Drawing her tongue into his mouth, he sucked, feasting on the spicy flavour of her mouth. She drew back, gasping for air, and, insatiable now, he hauled her back, claiming her mouth in a kiss that set every cell in his body clamouring for more.

Maybe this wasn't such a brilliant idea.

Thea, her senses aflame as never before; feeling she was losing control of the situation, something she purposefully never did, drew back, gasping for air. Only to be dragged ruthlessly back. Into a kiss that drove all conscious thought from her head.

Acting purely on instinct, she became a creature of fire, relentlessly craving more. Urgently, her hands raced over his torso.

Touching.

Stroking.

Finding their way inside his shirt. Where they discovered the heat and texture of aroused masculine flesh.

Encouraged by his throaty growls and tensing muscles, she flicked her thumb across the tight bud of a flat male nipple, eliciting a sharp hiss. Again.

Fiery passion overpowering reason, Thea's uneasy instinct for caution was drowned in the sea of sensation engulfing her.

Revelling in her feminine power, she sagged against him. Sinking to sit astride his thighs, she rubbed aching breasts against his chest. The steely rod of his erection rose, blatantly rampant between their bodies. Thea wriggled, seeking closer contact, but with her feet dangling just off the floor she lacked the necessary traction.

Lost control in their duel for supremacy.

Sanity beat desperate fists against Josh's baser instincts to throw the woman to the floor and give her what she demanded with every sinuous movement of her hot little body and greedy little hands.

Not until Ellie's voice uttered a decisive 'No!' in his brain did sanity gain the upper hand.

Drawing on strength he didn't know he had, Josh reared to his feet. At the last moment before she landed on the floor, he caught hold of Thea. Lifting her, he swung round and dumped her ignominiously onto the chair he'd been occupying. Gasping for breath, he leaned against the bench, supporting himself on trembling arms.

Mind a dizzying blank, Thea huddled on the chair where Josh had so unceremoniously dumped her.

Awareness of the present, and the very recent past, rapidly returning, Thea strove to make sense of what had just happened. One thing above all else stood clearly in her mind. Irrespective of whether or not she'd wanted what almost happened, she had been resoundingly rejected.

Dumped! Like a sack of potatoes!

Fighting tears, which if allowed to fall threatened to be unstoppable, she sat up straight, fussing over her clothes which were in an appalling state of disarray. Glancing sideways at the cause of her misery, she studied Josh's heaving shoulders and rasping breath.

Rejecting her hadn't come easy. It had cost him. A fact which gave her a small measure of satisfaction.

Rejection was humiliating enough. Easy rejection ... Well. That would have been unbearable.

Becoming aware he was under observation, Josh looked up. In the mirror he came eye-to-eye with a pouting Thea. Cheeks flushed with embarrassment, she stared defiantly back at him. Wholly unrepentant.

"Living dangerously, Thea," he growled.

Words to explain himself lost beyond layer upon layer of personally-imposed isolation from normal human interaction, he threw the blame back on her.

"So what? Maybe I like playing with fire. Maybe I don't care if I get burnt to a cinder," she muttered in reply, totally unprepared for his reaction.

What could be seen of Josh's face above the beard turned ashen. He grabbed her by the arms, pulling her to her feet and giving her a peremptory shake.

"Don't say that! Don't ever joke about getting burnt!"

He let her go, covering his face with his hands. A fine tremor shook his frame.

Startled, Thea placed a cautious hand lightly on his arm.

"Josh? Josh, what is it?" she whispered.

"Nothing. Nothing's wrong. I've got to go." He shook her off and blindly headed for the door.

Bewildered by the sudden emotional changes, Thea, floundered in his wake. Mouth agape, she stared after him, wondering exactly what was going on. This was more than a simple rejection.

The door already half closed behind him, Josh stuck his head back in.

"I'm sorry, Thea. I shouldn't have let things get so out of hand just now. Not your fault."

Well, that's generous of him.

Guiltily, she stared after him, all too aware she'd been the one who lit the spark. Then fanned it into a conflagration.

Ought I apologise to him?

Not on, she decided.

"I've got no right to be kissing anyone," Josh added. "Especially when she's not the right woman."

This time the door clicked shut behind him.

If I'm the wrong woman, why do I feel so certain he's the right bloody man?

~~~~~

An automaton with the sheen of unshed tears blurring her vision, Thea locked the front door of the salon behind Josh.

Refusing for the moment to confront the jumble of emotions unleashed by the humiliating episode, she restored her workplace to its pristine end-of-day readiness then retreated to her home behind the salon.

Aimlessly, she gravitated to the windows from which she looked across the yard to where a light shone on Josh Marten's side veranda. Looked across to where he appeared to be replacing the damaged floorboards.

A strange time for a job which he hadn't previously considered an urgent priority.

Resting her forehead against the glass, arms held tightly across her body, Thea stood in the dark, silently contemplating the enigma living next door. Calmer now, she allowed the recent events to replay in her mind. Yes, he'd soundly rejected her; and that hurt. Hurt like Hell. Because …

She forced herself to face, and accept, the hard truth. Just as in years past she'd forced herself to face and accept other hard truths. Truths even more painful, having, at the time, been without precedent in her young life.

When she kissed Josh tonight, she'd believed she was offering a tentative invitation to indulge themselves in mutually satisfying sex. A rare offer which had never previously been thrown back in her face.

Her breath huffed out. Shaking her head, she corrected her self-serving lie.

Who am I kidding? It was my heart I offered the infuriating damned man!

On a platter.

Sex was one thing, but her heart had never before been part of the equation. Until Josh Marten; and how she wished she could rewind her life and do things differently.

She shook violently, forced to free a hand to steady herself. Using both hands, Thea dashed away the moisture stinging her eyes. Wrenching the French doors open, she stumbled onto the patio, slumping down into her favourite of the pair of squatters' chairs she'd bought specially for that spot.

In brooding silence she watched Josh at his carpentering.

What can't be cured must be endured.

She recalled the favourite adage of her grandmother, usually uttered with Thea squarely in her tight-lipped sights.

Well, her heart was his, whether she wanted him to have it or not. Whether *he* wanted it or not; and the only cure which appealed to her was winning his in a fair exchange. To achieve that, she needed to know what made him tick.

Methodically, she considered all she'd learnt of Josh Marten. Which was surprisingly little, apart from his profession, and the mutual attraction which existed between them.

It is mutual, she assured herself. She wasn't mistaken in that, but she'd let herself be carried away by her own desire. Let herself be blinded to the unknown traumas which had led to his withdrawal into his present solitary existence.

That was the nub of it, she realised. From here she could do as he'd been telling her all along; and keep out of his way.

Slink away to lick her wounds in private.

Give up on him.

Or …

She could do what she ought to have done from the start; and hope she hadn't already carelessly squandered her chances. She sat up straighter in the chair, swinging her feet to the ground. Standing, she moved forward to lean against one of the roof supports, arms once again wrapped tightly around her body. Fixing her gaze on the object of her painful thoughts, she reviewed her preferred option again.

Slowly.

Carefully.

Wondering if she had what it took.

Deciding in the end she really had no other option at all. Not if she was ever to look upon herself with self-respect again.

It wouldn't be easy.

She'd be picking her way through a minefield with no guarantee of a safe passage to the other side, but if she made it through, surely the risk would be worth it.

Filled with new resolve, Thea went back inside to take the first step towards an uncertain future.

Seated in front of her laptop, she googled Josh Marten.

9

Eddie Patterson found Josh hard at work in his shed at eight-thirty the next morning. Unable to sleep for the combination of unsatisfied lust and painful memories unleased by his lapse with Thea, he'd sought refuge in work; fixing the veranda floorboards. When that failed to have the desired effect, he retreated to the shed. The piece he'd begun in the small hours of the morning bore a recognisable kinship to those tortured structures he'd created after Ellie.

Catching a shadowy glimpse of movement in the doorway, he set down his tools, surprised to see the sun was already half-way up the sky. Wearily removing his protective helmet, he brushed back sweat-damp hair and turned to confront the intruder.

Just what I need. Another annoying bloody woman.

An additional overlay of moroseness coloured his habitual terse greeting.

A moroseness blithely ignored by Eddie. She was on a mission; and didn't intend to take 'No' for an answer.

"Good morning, Josh. Pete told me you'll be away for a few days. I'm so glad I caught you before you left."

Resigned to his fate, Josh checked his watch, then gestured Eddie ahead of him towards the house. The structural repairs were almost completed, but the linings were still ripped out to allow access to the wiring and plumbing. The old farmhouse was barely liveable, but since the veranda was as far as Eddie would be getting, the shortcomings of the interior didn't matter a damn.

"Only just, Eddie. I'll make us a cuppa then you can tell me how I can help you." He hated encouraging her, but was in desperate need of strong coffee himself.

When he returned, his visitor was studying the dryad sculpture, making him wish he'd had the foresight to throw a dropcloth over it last night. He could do without being reminded at every turn of the woman who'd been its inspiration. The woman with whom he'd so nearly betrayed Ellie.

"Thank you, Dear." Eddie made herself comfortable then launched into her prepared spiel. "The local CWA has decided to host a special fund-raiser for the farmers who've been hard hit with this dreadful drought. We've settled on a concert with a monster raffle to be drawn on the night."

"And you'd like me to provide the monster?" Josh raised his brow, drily pre-empting her.

"Pretty much, Josh, Dear." It took more than Josh Marten to faze Eddie Patterson. "We've already got a nice collection of prizes, but I felt a tiny little genuine Josh Marten artwork might attract some extra money from out of town; and those struggling farmers need all the help we can give them."

She didn't really need to bring her compelling gaze into play. Josh didn't have a problem with supporting such a worthy cause. He was relieved that was all she wanted.

"Okay. Wait here and I'll go dig something up."

He headed back to the shed, leaving a beaming Eddie savouring her mug of coffee.

As she was leaving several minutes later, a quirky sheepdog pup constructed from spare parts under her arm, she nodded at the dryad.

"You've got Sophie down to a tee. Was she a commissioned piece, Josh? I wouldn't have thought either the Whitmans or Dot James could afford your fees for a life-size statue."

Startled, Josh looked from the sculpture to Eddie, then back again, seeing it through her eyes. Just in time, he snapped his mouth closed, keeping the truth to himself.

"I suppose it does look a bit like Sophie, not that I know her all that well. It's not her, though. It's what came out of the piece of wood when I began paring it down to expose the soul hidden inside it. It's a forest dryad to go in my garden when I get time to do a bit of landscaping."

After he'd waved Eddie off, Josh looked at Lunara with new insight. He'd thought from the first he'd seen Thea Benson's face before.

Now, thanks to Eddie, he knew who she reminded him of – both Dorothy James and her daughter Sophie. They must be the mysterious family Thea had been tracing. He wondered how close the relationship was. Even more, he wondered why she'd said nothing more about her search.

The truck to load the sculpture for the casino pulled in through the gate, its arrival driving his secretive neighbour from his mind.

~~~~~

Josh had been back from Sydney for a week; and hadn't spoken to Thea. Not once. He still felt uncomfortable with the way he'd treated her. She wasn't to know he was off-limits. Couldn't he have got his message across without being so … mean?

He felt mean. Every time he thought of her. Which was more often than he liked, since he couldn't give her what she wanted from him.

He'd seen her in her garden from time to time, but she'd never been looking his way, and although he couldn't tell for sure, it felt as if she was avoiding him. He ought to be pleased she'd taken his warning to heart. So why wasn't he?

He ought to be happy.

His sculpture for the casino had been given rave reviews, resulting in two new commissions and several possibles. The kind of success he'd been chasing for years was within his grasp.

He should be over the moon.

Instead, he was so cranky, if he'd had a cat he might have kicked it.

He'd reached that point in his misery-fest when a loud whistle brought his head round.

Thea Benson, the source of all his woes, stood on her side of the dividing fence between their properties, waving at him.

"Josh! Got a minute?"

What did she want? He had half a mind to ignore her. See how she liked a bit of her own back. Only, by the time his thoughts arrived at that point, his feet, acting on their own initiative, had carried him almost up to where she stood. Feeling a happy smile rising to his lips, he took himself sternly in hand, deepening his habitual scowl.

He wasn't happy she was finally taking notice of him. No way was he so fickle.

"What happened to the pink?"

He almost hadn't noticed her change of hair colour and style. To him she was simply Thea; her hair colour part of her outfit for the day.

"New month. New look." Thea ran her fingers self-consciously through her straight, slightly longer, neon-blue style. "That's not important. The thing is, Josh, Eddie asked me to give you this." She held out an envelope bearing his name.

"Eddie Patterson? What's she want now?"

He was tempted to chuck it in the bin, unopened, whatever it was, only Thea obviously expected a more appropriate response from him. He turned it over in his hands. Delaying.

"For God's sake, Josh. It won't bite. Open the damn thing."

"You don't know Eddie Patterson," he muttered. "She's always after something."

"Course she is. She's a woman who gets things done." Thea laughed, then seeing Josh was seriously uncomfortable, relented.

"You know, Josh, even though she's always chasing something up, I've never known her to be at all unkind, unlike other gossips. She's usually got someone's wellbeing in mind. I know I'd be on her doorstep like a shot if I was in trouble."

Josh stared at her, then, tacitly agreeing, ripped open the envelope, extracting a ticket to the concert being held on Saturday night. He frowned. Why was Eddie sending him a ticket? He'd given her a raffle prize. He'd bought a swag of raffle tickets from her table outside Pete Hackett's hardware shop only the other day. What more did the damn woman want?

About to tear it up, he caught Thea glaring at him and decided not to. Yet. Putting it in his pocket earned him one of her sunny smiles.

"You've given this fundraiser a real boost with your donation, Josh. It's created a lot of outside interest. People from all over are buying tickets in the hope of winning Bluey. Eddie just noticed you hadn't bought a concert ticket and didn't want you to miss out."

"I hadn't bought one because I'm not going."

"Oh, Josh." Thea gave him a lop-sided smile which made his heart stutter in his chest.

"It'll be fun. No-one will expect you to do anything except enjoy yourself. Joey Lambert and a couple of his mates have a skit guaranteed to have everyone rolling in the aisles. And if that's not incentive enough," she assumed a coy Betty Boop pose, fluttering her lashes at him, "I'm doing a simply fantastic song and dance routine."

She did a quick soft-shoe shuffle on the spot.

When he didn't jump in with an outright refusal, she pushed a bit harder. Eddie's instructions had been unequivocal. 'You see he comes, Thea, Dear. That boy needs prising out of his shell.'

While she wasn't at all sure Eddie had chosen the right emissary, she agreed wholeheartedly with the sentiment and determined to give the mission her best shot.

When she'd read his traumatic story online, she'd felt horribly guilty for forcing herself on him. She'd mistakenly thought all he needed was a nudge in the right direction.

Knowing what he'd suffered, was still suffering, didn't change how she felt about him. If anything, it strengthened her attachment. The difference now being that she'd vowed to give him all the space he needed to find his way back to the light in his own time. She'd simply be there for him and hope it was her he turned to when the day arrived that he put his grief behind him.

"Please Josh," she cajoled, abandoning every last hint of flirtatiousness to resort to outright begging.

Go!

Josh could resist Eddie's politely couched commands.

He could resist Thea's blandishments, although not as easily.

The one person he never resisted, had never attempted to resist, was Ellie; and it was her voice echoing in his mind.

He'd talked to her from the first. Silently when others were within earshot and out loud when he knew he was alone. He'd told her all the small happenings of his days. Discussed his work with her. Asked her advice.

The day she answered him, he'd sat in stunned silence for hours, reliving her gentle approval of his decision to leave Melbourne. Then she'd frustrated the Hell out of him by vetoing every place he'd looked at.

Until he hit on The Crossing. She hadn't exactly said she liked the old house on Murchison Lane when he saw it online, but he'd felt her nod of approval the day they came to view it.

After that, he'd have moved mountains to take possession. Only he hadn't needed to. The purchase had gone without a hitch. Which was something he'd gradually come to notice about Ellie's rare communications.

If he heeded her advice, his life flowed evenly; but if he tried going his own stubborn way, he ran into no end of snags. The pile of twisted wreckage in the back of the shed was testament to that.

Only, just lately, Ellie had begun to sound as if she'd been talking to Eddie Patterson; and he didn't like it. Over this issue of attending the concert, she'd gone too far, and so he told her.

No.

No bolt from the blue was hurled to strike him down, but he'd swear he felt the silent vibration of a mental door being slammed in his face. He closed his eyes. And stood his ground. Against Ellie, and Thea. Especially against Eddie. When he spoke to Thea, he spoke to all three of them.

"No thanks, Thea. You can tell Eddie Patterson amateur theatricals aren't my cup of tea."

He thrust the ticket back into her hands and strode off to his house. His refuge from interfering women.

Ellie would come around. She'd never been one to hold a grudge. He hoped she wouldn't stay away too long, though. Already he missed her, feeling the chill of her withdrawal.

"It's not about the quality of the entertainment, you know," Thea yelled after him, interrupting the self-inflicted misery of his thoughts.

"It's about giving people a chance to be generous to those in need."

Josh felt the door that had slammed shut in his mind ease open a fraction, as if Ellie was standing there, listening for his answer.

Thea made a good point.

"I'll think about it," he compromised, without slowing his escape.

Please, my Darling.

Ellie accompanied her plea with the irresistible feel of her warm, capable arms wrapped around his shoulders. He'd not felt her presence so strongly since …

Josh caved.

"Okay. I'll be there," he yelled, from the bottom of his steps.

"You'll need this, then." Thea waved the ticket in the air, scrambled over the fence, and raced after him.

"You won't regret it," she promised, shoving the envelope into his hands. Eyes glowing, she reached up and hugged him; then afraid of stirring up an emotional hornet's nest, she ran back again, giving him a last wave as she crossed the fence and headed into her own domain.

I like her.

Me too, Ellie, even though I shouldn't.

Standing in the hot sun at the foot of his steps, Josh felt the imprint of two pairs of arms holding him. And couldn't tell which was which.

~~~~~

Expecting to be allowed to hide in a back corner, Josh was disconcerted when the youthful usher who checked his ticket personally escorted him to a seat in the front row. Len Woodcock and his wife, Mili, occupied chairs to his left, with Dot James and the Whitmans to his right. Sophie and Bob were up from Canberra, he noted. He'd tried to argue his placement with the usher, but shut his mouth when Len shook his hand.

"Glad I caught you tonight, Josh. I think I'm onto some of that antique furniture you were looking for. There's a house clearance over in Gundagai next week. Come in on Monday and we'll go through the auction catalogue. The period you're after's not exactly flavour of the month, so we might be able to pick it up quite reasonably."

"Hello Josh." Dot greeted him from the other side. "Wasn't it lovely of Eddie to reserve the front rows for those of us who donated prizes?"

Sit down and be grateful, Ellie whispered, so he sat where he'd been told.

A tap on the shoulder had him turning to the row behind where the Morgan family claimed a block of seats.

"Love your Bluey," Barbara Morgan whispered.

She cast a quick glance to where her husband was deep in conversation with Bill Whitman. Lowering her voice to a conspiratorial whisper, she added, "If we don't win him, I'll be out to your shed to buy one like him for Andrew's seventieth birthday that's coming up. He breeds kelpies, you know, and I reckon it's the perfect present for him. Don't you, Angie?" She turned to her daughter-in-law for corroboration.

Josh made a mental note to make a new litter of pups. They'd become one of his signature pieces while he struggled to make ends meet while waiting to be discovered, and were still among his favourites.

The lights dimmed, and with a great deal of rustling, the audience settled into their seats. Eddie appeared in a spotlight at the front of the stage, and invited their local MHR, Robert Whitman to say a few words.

"Make sure it's only a few, Laddie," hooted Matt Hendersen from midway down the auditorium.

With a laugh, Bob did just that, briefly but sincerely thanking everyone for their support and hard work in aid of drought relief for the farmers.

"Your money already has hay being rolled out across the North-West to those who need it," he concluded, "and now it's your turn to reap the rewards. Eddie has asked me to draw the first of the raffle prizes. If you need more tickets, they're on sale at the table by the front door. And now for the first of a ton of prizes." He spun the barrel, then reached in to extract a winner.

"Tom Carey, you get coffee and cake courtesy of the Tans. Now, let's get this show on the road."

Ted Lanner, emcee for the night, combined a dry sense of humour with an unerring grasp on local and national affairs which earned him as many laughs from his parochial audience as any professional comedian could hope for. He kept the acts on schedule, drawing more prizes whenever a change of scenery slowed things down. So far Josh had counted more than twenty small prizes, including vouchers to be redeemed at Thea's salon, all going to different winners.

The schoolchildren who'd led the steady parade of acts had been pretty much what he'd expected, except for one little girl who appeared to be a star in the making. He hoped she'd come on again. He'd enjoyed her rendition of *The Drover's Dream*, backed by her classmates playing the animals.

A couple of times he'd had to stifle a yawn, but he was definitely in the minority. Even the most bumbling of ballerinas had enough family support to leave the stage beaming with pride.

"Hang in there, Mate," Len whispered sympathetically from behind his hand.

"The best acts are after the interval. I hear that cute little hairdresser is pretty good. She's certainly easy on the eye."

And why that comment raised his hackles, Josh couldn't fathom. Thea Benson *was* easy on the eye. Whatever the colour of her hair, and he'd noted another change. Today she sported rainbow stripes.

The last act before the interval featured Joey Lambert and his friends doing a slapstick dramatization of Banjo Patterson's *Man From Ironbark*.

"Old Banjo's no relation to our Mike," whispered Len, surprising Josh, who hadn't thought for a moment that he was.

If they didn't exactly have the hugely partisan crowd rolling in the aisles, at least everyone, Josh included, laughed at their antics.

"Eddie's a good producer, isn't she Josh?" Dot turned to her neighbour with a smile. "She knows to send them off to the interval in a good mood. Then they'll loosen their purse-strings at the kiosk. If we're lucky, we'll sell more raffle tickets as well. There's still a lot of prizes to go. And that's my cue. I'm manning the raffle table along with Sophie and Hazel."

Not having won anything yet, Josh good-naturedly took the hint and lined up for more tickets, then paid his gold coin for coffee and a cookie, lucky enough to snaffle one of the home baked gingernuts that were going fast. Not wanting to get roped into conversation, he found a quiet corner to prop up the wall and crowd-watch till it was time to return for the second half.

He refused to admit it, but his pulse rate rose in expectation of Thea's song and dance number.

He almost didn't recognise her at first.

Backed by a troupe of cloaked and masked boys and girls, she performed a modern ballet similar to the one she'd been practising the day he'd fronted her about the volume of her music. If he hadn't seen her dancing in her back room, he might not have recognised her, but now her firmly rounded, lycra-clad figure moved in a distinctive manner he'd know anywhere.

Apart from the mop of rainbow hair she'd obviously adopted as part of her costume.

What about her song and dance act? He wondered.

She'll be on again, Ellie's voice answered.

And she was. Entering for the second-last act, she tapped her demure way to centre stage, dressed in a flapper era costume and twirling a parasol. The music segued smoothly into the Gershwin classic, *Someone to Watch Over Me.*

Low and husky, Thea's voice resonated within Josh's body, her eyes flirting with his as she sang and danced her way across the stage and back again. When she concluded by blowing him a kiss, he ran his finger round an already loose collar hoping no-one else was noticing how she singled him out.

Let one of The Crossing's stalwart ladies get a hold of that, he thought, *and it'll be round the town in a flash. It won't be just Eddie sticking her nose into my business. Snooping around and asking questions. It's enough to make a man up sticks and go bush for a week or two.*

He wondered idly what the fishing was like down the coast.

Then there was no time for thought.

Thea skipped down the side steps and, taking him by the hand, urged him up onto centre stage. With Len and Dot egging her on, he was left with no option other than going along with her.

"You're an absolutely fantastic audience," she carolled, holding her hands wide, laughing as she was given a resounding cheer. Taking Josh by the hand again, she called out, "How about one of those lovely cheers for Oxley Crossing's very own world-famous sculptor." An even louder cheer echoed from the rafters of the old hall.

"He's a bit of a recluse, you know, so he probably hates me for dragging him up here. Hope he'll be a sport about it." A roar of laughter greeted this behind-her-hand aside to the audience.

Not much I can bloody well do after the way she ambushed me.

Anger more than embarrassment tinged Josh's cheeks with red.

"Last raffle draw of the night, folks, and Eddie reckoned Josh here ought to do the honours." Thea had passed the microphone back to Ted, who continued in his hearty style. "Who's going to take Bluey home with them tonight?"

Thea wheeled the barrel back on stage, and Eddie appeared, the metal pup cradled in her arms, to stand between Josh and Ted. Mutely, Josh reached into the barrel and withdrew a scrunched-up slip of paper. He handed it to Ted who made a big production out of unfolding it and peering around the audience.

"Is Josie Tan here?" he asked, answered by an ear-splitting squeal.

"Here I am, Mr Lanner. Did I really win Bluey?"

"Really and truly, young lady. Up you come to collect him."

As Joseph Tan helped his granddaughter down from the stage with her prize, the entire cast filed in, leading the audience in a rousing rendition of *I Still Call Australia Home*. Followed by the National Anthem, it signalled the end of the evening's entertainment, and people began streaming out the door.

Thea, her arm linked with his, still anchoring Josh at her side, sighed and yawned.

"It's been tremendous fun, but I'm exhausted. Want a lift, Josh? I brought the car to carry my costumes home."

"Okay."

With her body pressed closely against his side, her well-remembered perfume clouding his senses, all Josh could think of was how much he wanted to taste her again. To savour the unique, slightly peppery flavour of her mouth beneath his. Sometime during the last ten minutes he'd lost sight of why that was such a bad idea.

10

To Josh's mind, the silence in the car possessed a fraught quality he found vaguely unnerving, probably because of the unfamiliar direction his thoughts were taking him. Casting around for a safe topic of conversation to carry them over till they arrived at Thea's place, safely out of sight of prying eyes, he blurted out,

"You seemed to be the flavour of the month back there."

Glancing sideways, Thea gave an almost imperceptible shrug.

"I like people. I make an effort to be friendly and helpful; unlike someone I'll leave unnamed." She waited a moment, but when Josh didn't rise to her bait, she continued. "My salon offers a useful service to this town, so it's also good for business to be involved in the community. You ought to try it, you know. They're nice people here in The Crossing."

Not such a safe topic after all, he thought, moving on.

"You were lucky you could arrange the financing at short notice when Toni decided to sell up."

Another shrug which went unseen in the dark.

Tempted to tell her inquisitor to mind his own business, Thea relented. Josh was in a strange mood tonight. Not as locked away within himself as usual. Almost mellow, he'd given every appearance of enjoying the show.

Maybe if I open up to him, he'll reciprocate.

"My parents left money in a trust fund," she answered, buoyed by hope. "I'd been thinking of buying my own salon for quite a while."

"How long is 'quite a while'?" Josh was really only avoiding giving her the opportunity to ask searching questions of her own, but her answer made him sit up and take notice.

"The trust was wound up when I turned twenty-five, but I'd always known the money was coming to me, so I'd have to say, owning my own business has been on the backburner since I decided on a career in hairdressing. Sometime in my mid-teens, at best guess. Of course, I had to learn my trade first, and get a bit of experience under my belt," she elaborated, to be shocked by his response.

"Good God, Woman," he burst out. "You're hardly brimming with ambition, are you? If I'd had access to money, I'd have set myself up immediately. Then maybe we wouldn't have been living in a rented firetrap; and maybe Ellie ..." Shocked at what he'd almost let slip, Josh shut up like a clam.

Thea cruised to a stop in her carport, but Josh, lost in unhappy memories, made no move to open his door. Curious, she turned in her seat to study him. From her online research, she'd learned his wife, Ellie, had died in a house fire.

A bit over two years ago, if she remembered rightly. Leaving him to his memories, Thea quietly set about collecting her things from the backseat. Ready to go inside, she touched his arm lightly, bringing him back to the present.

"Coming in? I'll put the kettle on."

Having regained control, his mind now mercifully blank, Josh heaved himself out of Thea's small car and followed. His earlier desires had been effectively quenched, but still, he didn't fancy being alone right now. Afraid Thea would pick up on his slip and start poking around in his past, he got in first, reverting to their previous conversation.

"How come you didn't look for a salon somewhere in Sydney? You'd have been closer to your friends."

"I did look at a few places," she answered, "but the rents were horrendous, and nothing felt right."

"How old were you when your parents died?"

"Nine."

"That's young to be on your own. I suppose you had family who took you in?"

Busy holding his own thoughts at bay, Josh failed to take note of Thea's growing tension.

Using tea-making as an excuse to turn her back, Thea gritted her teeth and breathed deep, reaching into her mind for the place she went when the world crowded in on her. If it hadn't been for her hope of a fair exchange of confidences, leading to a step forward in their relationship, she'd have changed the subject.

"I was hurt in the accident. When I was ready to go home from hospital, the social worker sat me down and explained that I had been adopted. First I'd heard of it. The rest of them, Dad's family, didn't want me because I 'wasn't their blood'." Voice betraying the bitterness she still felt towards those grandparents and aunt who'd abandoned her like an unwanted Christmas pet, she added the air-parenthesis with her index fingers.

"All I had left was the trust fund. I guess while it was intact, I felt my parents were still looking out for me. Maybe that's why it took so long to buy my salon. Or maybe I'm just lacking ambition, like you said."

She abruptly picked up the tray and strode with it onto the patio.

Scrambling to process the information dump he'd unleashed, Josh followed slowly in her wake. He'd had a raw deal from life, but he'd been an adult when he lost Ellie. And nothing that happened to him involved a sickening betrayal by his family. He couldn't imagine how that must have felt for a sensitive, already grieving child.

Nine! Christ almighty!

He silently shook his head. Sipping his tea in silence, he absorbed the ramifications.

How on earth had Thea Benson turned out the cheerful extrovert she was, charming everyone who crossed her path? Could it be an act to hide her pain? At least in part? Look how a few simple questions had opened up old hurts. While Josh pondered, Thea was simply relieved at his forbearance.

She sipped her tea, gradually feeling her equilibrium restoring itself.

Of course!

Josh began putting together disparate pieces of the puzzle that was Thea Benson. She'd claimed to have come in search of family, but …

Not her adoptive family. They'd rejected her. Which left her birth family!

"She's your mother, isn't she?" Josh almost shouted in his excitement at solving the riddle. "Dot James is your birth mother; making Sophie your sister! You must be so happy to have found them, Thea. They're good people, not like those other mean bastards. You know, I'd have thought news like this would have been all over town, ages ago, but I haven't heard a whisper."

"I haven't told them."

There was the crackle of thin ice in Thea's distant tones, but Josh wasn't listening. He blundered on.

"Not told … Why not, for God's sake?"

"You said it yourself, Josh. They're nice people. They've got standing in The Crossing. There'd be gossip. They wouldn't like it. Besides," and, from her viewpoint, this was the crux of the issue.

"Dot didn't want me when I was born. Why do you imagine she'd feel differently now?"

Josh gaped at her, his mouth working soundlessly for several seconds.

"You're scared she'll have nothing to do with you, aren't you? And that's why you haven't told her." He shook his head in disbelief.

"I never took you for a coward, Thea. That poor woman probably had no choice back then. She'd have been just a bit of a kid herself. At the very least, I imagine she'd be relieved to know you're okay."

That poor woman! Government allowances made it possible for girls to keep their babies. If they wanted to. Since then she's had plenty of time to trace me if she was concerned about me.

A strangled gasp, almost a sob, burst from Thea's throat.

Besides, what about me? Don't my feelings count?

But Josh wasn't finished with her yet.

He picked up her hand, gently stroking the clenched fingers until they opened up. Belatedly realising he'd opened up a can of worms, he deliberately spoke as soothingly as he could.

"You really ought to tell her, Thea. You owe her that much, and the longer you leave it, the harder it'll be. I promise you; you'll feel better when you do."

"Not if she doesn't want to know," Thea muttered, stubbornly refusing to back down. She had only just begun to build a tenuous friendship with the woman who'd given birth to her. Everything within her resisted jeopardising that relationship.

And, anyway, just who was Josh Marten to tell her what she should or shouldn't do?

Or how she ought to feel?

Faced with tragedy, he'd locked his emotions away and cut himself off from family and friends. He didn't even care enough to … But she halted her thoughts at that point. She wasn't going there. No way.

"I'm too tired to think about all this tonight, Josh."

Even as she denied it, Thea recognised the truth of Josh's accusation. Recognised she was doing it again, taking the coward's way out. Refusing to face up to the situation.

Just as she'd been doing ever since she'd learnt the truth of her parentage. But, coward's way or not, she simply couldn't take any more of his probing questions.

Standing up, she stacked the dirty cups back on the tray, giving Josh no option but to leave.

"He's a great one to talk," she muttered bitterly to herself as she prepared for bed. "At least I'm not sticking my head in the sand, pretending I'm no longer part of the human race. I'm getting on with my life."

She'd bared her soul; and been called a coward for her pains. Been put in the wrong. She wouldn't be in a hurry to share her darkest secrets in future.

Not with anyone.

Certainly not with Josh Bloody Marten who was more concerned with Dot's feelings than hers. Let him heal himself before he started on her.

She hoped she didn't cross trails with him again any time soon. She wasn't even sure how she felt about him after tonight's inquisition. If asked, she'd probably claim to hate the sight of him.

Which somehow failed to settle the churning in her gut for something lost before it had properly begun. Something which so nearly might have been.

She couldn't still want a crass idiot who'd got the wrong end of the stick, and despised her for being a coward.

Could she?

~~~~~

Tossing and turning as sleep eluded him, shame for the way he'd thought to relieve the sexual itch Thea aroused in him, made Josh want to atone, even though the moment had been lost and nothing had happened.

The poor kid had been through the wringer. Instead of being used as he'd been about to, she deserved a man who'd love and cherish her. Knowing it could never be him, didn't diminish his unfamiliar urge to protect. Although, he thought, he might be able to manage friendship.

He'd damn well better be up to it; Thea needed a friend who understood the pain gnawing away at her. A friend willing to stand at her back if the ladies of The Crossing gave her a hard time when they learned the truth. Which they would, sooner or later.

If he'd learnt one thing since arriving in The Crossing, it was that no secrets stayed buried forever.

11

The kookaburras were stirring in the ancient, gnarled river redgums down by the creek, but Thea pulled the pillow over her head, not yet ready to face the day. An hour later the pillow landed with a muffled thump against the door of her closet. She yawned and stretched, slowly sitting up, her head resting heavily on her knees.

Thank goodness it's Sunday!

Tossing and turning fitfully, she hadn't got much sleep, her mind spinning and spinning from one uncomfortable subject to another like a hamster on a wheel; but somewhere in the wee, small hours she'd finally straightened out her muddled thoughts. Her emotions were once again reined in.

Under control.

She'd been getting soft since moving to The Crossing, allowing foolish daydreams to blind her to the hard truths she'd always known. It had taken too long to learn not to put her happiness in the hands of other people for her to jeopardise the hard-won composure with which she faced the world every day.

Daydreams always resulted in disappointment when exposed to cold reality. Well, she'd be indulging in no more such foolishness! It felt good to once again be her familiar hard-nosed realistic self.

In control.

She didn't need Dot James. Or Josh Marten. Didn't need anyone. At all.

If she repeated it often enough, she might even believe it.

Although, ...

Josh had been right when he called her a coward. Whatever her own concerns, Dorothy James must be warned before some observant denizen of Oxley Crossing blurted out a difficult-to-answer question, catching her on the hop. Having chosen to alter the status quo by moving to Oxley Crossing, she, Thea, did owe Dot that much.

Sooner being better than later; safer; she'd do it today. No more procrastinating. And there'd be no sentimentality about it!

A hot shower washed most of the cobwebs away, but if she was to successfully fulfil the difficult task she had assigned to this day, she needed a caffeine boost.

Suspecting one cup wouldn't suffice, she made up a pot and took it through to her favourite chair on the back patio, nearly tripping over the life-size metal echidna sitting on the mat as if about to clamber over the shallow step and push his way inside.

Putting her breakfast tray down, she scooped him up, turning over the label round his neck to read the neatly lettered message.

I'm prickly, but I care.

JM

Not that she needed the swirling initials at the bottom to tell her it was from Josh; its workmanship proclaimed its origins.

Simple, but to the point, his words warmed the cold, hard ball in her gut where she'd locked down her feelings for the dratted man, telling herself she was done with him. With a weak chuckle, she read the message again, knuckling away the moisture gathering in her eyes.

It eased the burden to know he cared about her. It shouldn't; but it did.

"Well, Mr Prickles," Thea held the small sculpture up, studying it eye-to-eye, "I guess this means I'm going to have to give your creator another chance, but I'm telling you straight; anything more than friendship is up to him. Man-chasing doesn't suit me. Especially when the man doesn't want to be caught."

With her new friend, Mr Prickles, sitting on the table in front of her, she ran over her mental to-do list.

Thanking Josh was now slotted in after lunch. There was a more urgent item heading the list, and if she didn't hurry up, she'd be late. Dot James usually attended the ten o'clock morning service, and she'd need time to take in what was about to be landed in her lap.

If Thea wasn't so nervous, she'd have been feeling smug.

Just let Josh Marten call her a coward again!

Quickly clearing away her breakfast dishes, she collected the folder containing the report from Alexis Jones. Before she could chicken out and change her mind, she marched down the road, across the bridge, and in at the door of the newsagents, coming to an abrupt halt when she there was no sign of her quarry.

"Hi Jean. Dot not here?"

"Oh, hello Thea. Loved your performance last night. Good enough to be a professional, you are. Gave our little concert a bit of class."

Impatience almost had Thea dancing on the spot, but she reined it in and answered Jean with a smile.

"I've had a fair bit of practice, Jean. I belonged to an amateur musical theatre group in Sydney and took dance classes every week for years."

"Maybe you could start up a group here. I'm sure you'd have plenty of takers." Finally, Jean remembered Thea's question, and continued, "Dot's not coming in today. I'll let you out the back door if you need to catch up with her. There you go," she suited her actions to her words, ushering Thea out through the office to the door into the courtyard. "Just go knock on her door. I know she's still at home."

"Thanks."

Thea smiled at Jean, and slowly made her way across the courtyard.

Nerves tied her stomach in knots, and if it hadn't been for Jean propping up the shop door behind her, idle curiosity clearly visible on her cheerful face, Thea felt she might have turned tail and run for home.

She wasn't at all sure she was going about this the right way, but the truth was, she hadn't been able to think of anything better.

Too soon for second thoughts, Dot opened the door.

"Why, Thea. How lovely to see you. I didn't have time to tell you last night how much I enjoyed the show. Eddie is over the moon at how successful it was."

"Eddie did a wonderful job putting it all together so quickly." Tempted to talk longer about the show, Thea took a bracing breath and plunged right in without any preamble.

"I'm not here to talk about the show, Dot. There's something I need to share with you. It might be better if you sit down before you read this."

She nudged the bewildered older woman into a chair and placed the folder in her hands.

"Thea? What's this?"

Without waiting for an answer Dot opened the cover and began reading Alexis Jones' summary of the report, her eyes immediately blurring with unshed tears. Like a naughty schoolkid fronting the principal, Thea shuffled guiltily from one foot to the other, watching her.

Maybe I shouldn't have sprung it on her so suddenly, she thought. *Maybe I should just get out of here.*

"Mum! Yoohoo."

Sophie, her husband Rob hard on her heels, bustled in before Dot reached the bottom of the page, but she'd read enough to get the gist of it.

"Mum, I hope you're sitting down. I've got fantastic news for you."

By then she was over the threshold and could see her mother was indeed sitting down. With silent tears streaming down her face. And Thea Benson looking guilty as Hell, edging towards the open door.

"Hold on, Thea!" Sophie grabbed her by the arm, preventing her get-away.

"Mum, what's the matter? What's upset you?"

"You're right, Sophie Darling. It's wonderful news. The best. I'm not upset at all. I'm happy. So happy." With that she burst into noisy sobs.

"I think I'd better go and leave you to it," Thea muttered, making another attempt at escape. This time unwittingly foiled by Robert, who'd noticed Jean's avid attention, and smartly closed the door, leaning against it. With a subdued huff of laughter, he decided to give his wife a helping hand.

"If all you happy ladies sit down, I'll put the kettle on. I guarantee you'll be needing a cuppa shortly. You too, Thea. What Sophie's discovered concerns you, too."

None of the three paid him the slightest heed, yet in no time at all they were gathered round the kitchen table, Dot drying her eyes with the tissue Sophie handed to her.

"Sophie, you won't believe what just happened. It's like a miracle." Dot beamed through the tearstains. "I've found Laura!"

"I know. That's what I came home this weekend to tell you, only we arrived too late last night so I waited till this morning."

"That's right, Dot," laughed Robert, slinging an arm around his wife's shoulders. "She was so excited, she didn't get a wink of sleep. Which means I didn't either. But how did you know? We haven't told you yet."

"How did you know? I only just found out when Thea showed me this." Dot waved the folder she'd been clutching to her chest.

"Thea found my Laura, and guess what?"

"Thea is Laura!" Sophie and Rob exclaimed together.

The next moment Thea was wrapped around by two pairs of feminine arms while Rob's grin from where he leaned against the kitchen bench rivalled the Cheshire Cat's.

It was all too much.

Thea could face cold rejection with dry-eyed stoicism, but open-hearted acceptance shattered her.

Dot's tears had been sun-showers filtered through the rainbow of her beaming smile.

Thea's were hard. Bitter. Dredged up from the bottom of her heart where she'd buried all the grief and loneliness of her long-ago abandonment. A lifetime's worth of pent-up tears she'd prided herself on never shedding, flooded out as if they'd go on flowing forever.

Dot simply held her. Pressing her head against her shoulder, she patted her back, murmuring soothing platitudes as if comforting a baby.

The baby she'd lost.

12

It was past five o'clock before Thea trudged across the unkempt yard and up the three freshly repaired steps to Josh's veranda, feeling it had been forever since she'd set out across the bridge into town early that morning.

"Hi Thea. I was looking for you earlier. Sorry if I upset you last night. It wasn't intentional if I did." Josh came across from his shed and climbed the short flight of steps at her side.

She flicked an upward glance towards where he stood watching her reaction to his apology, taking her time about answering.

Last night was so long ago she had to work to recall what he was talking about.

"You didn't upset me," she murmured, eyes lowered to the freshly sanded floorboards.

Then, more assertively, more clearly recalling her grievances against him the previous evening, she looked him up and down, adding, "You were wrong, though, when you called me a coward."

Taking a deep breath, Thea continued fiercely issuing her challenge.

"Being cautious, and, I'll admit, a little bit scared, doesn't make me a coward. It makes me sensible. You know Josh, fools rush in and all that." This time when she turned her face in his direction, she locked eyes, daring him to contradict her.

A self-conscious chuckle escaped his lips as he took in her pugnacious expression. She looked like a girl spoiling for a fight. Which she wasn't getting from him. A fight was the very last thing he wanted from this feisty woman.

"Steady on there, Thea. I never called you a coward. I distinctly remember saying I didn't think you were."

His hair-splitting set her lips twitching, her posture easing as she claimed one of his comfortable squatters' chairs, without waiting for an invitation. Josh lowered himself to his haunches in front of her, lifting her chin to examine her face. A frown creasing his forehead, he focused on her eyes.

"You've been crying," he observed, noting the reddened rims she hadn't been able to disguise. His frown deepened.

"Who's been giving you a hard time, Thea? Tell me and I'll go sort him out for you."

"That's a change of image. From curmudgeonly hermit to knight errant." This time it was Thea who chuckled.

"For Heaven' sake Josh. Sit down. There's no-one who needs 'sorting out'."

Josh pulled his chair round, perching on the edge so he could watch her as they talked.

"From the look of you, you've had a pretty hard day." He leaned forward, taking her hand in his.

The feel of his large, calloused palms protectively enfolding her much smaller hand felt so right; so perfect; it was almost Thea's undoing. Especially when he added, in a soft growl which sent tingles up her spine,

"If you need a friend, Thea, I'm here for you."

If I need a friend … Seems today is all about new connections. Thea dug in her pocket for a tissue to wipe her eyes.

"Thanks Josh. As it happens, a friend is exactly what I need right now. What you said last night spurred me into action. I knew I ought to tell Dot the truth. Sooner or later. After what you said last night, today seemed like the day. You've guessed, and several times Jean's commented that I remind her of someone. Eddie's been giving me funny looks too."

"Eddie!" Josh snorted, latching onto the last-mentioned person. "Let her get a whiff of this and it'll be all over town in a flash."

"It's going to be, anyway. Seems Dot's always wanted to find her lost baby, only she was too intimidated to do anything about it. She's planning to shout the news from the rooftops and is recruiting Eddie to help her put a good spin on it." Thea looked at Josh, wonder lighting up her eyes.

"I thought she'd want to make up a plausible story to account for our likeness without saying who I really am. Was sure she wouldn't want to acknowledge me."

The tissue was employed again.

"I was wrong, Josh. She fell on my neck, crying about how happy she was to have found her Laura again. I didn't know what to do. Then Sophie showed up, and …"

By the time Thea finished her recital of the day's momentous events, the tears had gone from leaking to streaming. Josh scooped her up and sat cradling her on his knees. Her wet face pressed into his shoulder, he rocked, patting her back and shushing her till her sobs reduced to sniffles.

Lasting in reality for only a minute or two, it felt to Thea like an eternity. A warm, secure eternity.

A loving eternity.

It felt too good to be true.

Like Dot's response earlier in the day.

She wasn't accustomed to such unquestioning acceptance.

Reluctantly, she extricated herself from the strong arms holding her within their safe embrace, seeking the bolstering chill of reality.

She couldn't afford a moment more of being so horribly vulnerable, regardless of how good it felt.

Standing securely on her own two feet once again, Thea began digging through her pockets for a fresh tissue. Not finding one, she swiped her eyes with the heel of her hand, then resorted to using the tail of her shirt to dry her face. She dredged up a wobbly smile for Josh.

"It's okay. I'm all right now. I'm just finding all this happy families stuff a bit much. Keep thinking I'll wake up and find they've changed their minds about me. You know Josh?"

Thea took a moment to consider her words before she spoke.

"I thought my father … biological father, must have abused Dot, for a lovely woman like her to give up her baby; but turns out it was *her* father who was the monster."

"Her Old Man was a real asswipe, 'scuse the French," Josh muttered angrily. "Imagine stealing his daughter's baby and selling it, then brainwashing her into thinking she'd committed some sort of unforgiveable sin. From what I've heard," he added, "that husband of hers was another bigoted bastard of the same kind. Bit like those relatives of yours who chucked you out to fend for yourself, I reckon."

Josh shoved his hands in his pockets and looked Thea over from where he was now leaning against the veranda railing.

She's one strong little cookie, he mused, *but she's not as tough as she thinks.* He pulled his hands out of his pockets, pushing himself fully erect.

"I was going to offer you a cuppa, Thea, but I reckon we both need something stronger."

"God yes," Thea almost moaned. "Make mine a very large glass of full-bodied red if you have it. If not, I'll nip home for a bottle."

"Actually, I was thinking more of scotch, but red will do."

He hurried off to investigate the contents of the cardboard carton in the corner of his kitchen which currently served as a bar. Meanwhile, Thea borrowed his bathroom to wash her face thoroughly and stuff a handful of tissues in her pocket. Just in case.

Seemed it was the sort of day she might need them again, though she hoped to God she was through crying. She never cried, yet today she'd shed enough tears to end the drought.

"There you go." Josh handed her a generously filled glass. They sat side by side in a silence that eased into companionable as the wine went down; so fast it was almost an insult to the excellence of the McLaren Vale shiraz. *Bygone Era,* Thea read on the label. Worth remembering next time she was in the bottle-shop.

Draining the last mellow drop, Thea turned to Josh with a smile.

"Thanks. I really needed that. Days like today, caffeine simply isn't enough."

Josh grinned back, offering a refill, but Thea shook her head, rising to her feet.

"I've been thinking, Josh. I've got a lasagne waiting to go in the oven. Plenty for two if you'd care to join me?"

"Better than the leftovers on toast I was planning to heat up." He got up to follow her across to her house, glad she seemed more her normal self again.

"Don't forget the bottle," Thea called over her shoulder. "What's left of that shiraz will be perfect with dinner."

13

Crossing her patio, Thea stopped to pat Mr Prickles, turning to Josh with a self-conscious laugh.

"You know? I went over to your place to thank you for Mr Prickles here, but I got sidetracked into talking about my affairs. Thank you, Josh. I absolutely love him."

"Thought he'd feel at home with you," Josh tried to brush her thanks aside. "I like my critters to go to good homes."

Laughing, the two of them stepped into the kitchen to share the dinner preparations.

Conversation over dinner was determinedly cheerful; touching on current affairs, movies, literature and Josh's recent trip to Sydney.

Anything, in fact except Thea's affairs.

It wasn't until they were settled, port in hand and classical music playing softly in the background, that Josh tackled the elephant in the room head-on.

"You know, Thea," he began tentatively, "with your ebullient nature, I would have imagined you'd be over the moon, with Dot taking you to her bosom and welcoming you as her long-lost child?"

Thea swirled the liqueur in her glass, eyeing him obliquely. She took a sip, sat up, tucking one foot beneath her, and squarely met his curious gaze.

"It's not that easy, Josh. I am happy. Happy tears happy. This is something I never dared dream could happen for me, but at the same time, I'm terrified." She pushed her hair back from her face, wondering how to explain so he'd understand her ambivalence.

"See Josh, I've spent most of my life believing there was some terrible reason nobody wanted me. Like my father being a murderer, or my parents in jail for something really, really bad. Because if that wasn't the case, why did no-one want me? I may come across as an optimistic air-head, but the bottom line is, I'm a rock-solid realist. I've had to be to survive. I never let myself indulge in 'What ifs' because I had no substance to build daydreams on."

Sipping again, she retreated into her thoughts.

Josh frowned, trying to imagine a life so bleak a child couldn't even dream of something better. It rivalled the grief-stricken depression he'd fallen into when Ellie left him.

Only, he felt ashamed to admit, *Thea handled it better than I did.*

A little shudder ran up Thea's spine, and she once again turned her attention to her companion.

"Today I was so sure Dot wouldn't want anything to do with me, I felt I was caught up in a tornedo when her reaction was the exact opposite. It was the most wonderful thing that's ever happened to me, yet I couldn't believe it at first. Even now, part of me is afraid it won't last; but you know, Josh? I want Dot and Sophie in my life. I want to be happy. I am happy," she stated vehemently.

"And every time I tell myself so, it becomes more real. No-one's taking my family away from me again."

Her belligerent look was back again, Josh noted.

"Good for you, Thea," he said, gruff-voiced. "I believe it's the real deal, too. Relax, and let Dot and Sophie love you. Be happy."

He put his empty glass on the table. Rising to his feet, he leaned over and kissed her on the cheek, setting shivers tingling down to Thea's toes.

"I'd better be going. Thanks for dinner. I've enjoyed this evening."

Is that it?

Thea stared at him in disbelief.

She'd been so sure tonight was leading up to more than an abrupt thanks for dinner, and an injunction to have a good life.

Josh turned and had almost made it to the door when Thea caught up with him.

She lay her hand on his shoulder, halting him.

"The evening doesn't have to be over yet, Josh."

He turned to her, an uncertain frown creasing his forehead

The words he intended to utter were lost when Thea slid both arms around his neck and rose onto her toes to kiss him on the mouth.

A long, warm, tacit invitation of a kiss.

An invitation she repeated in a whisper Josh barely heard, but which resounded through his heart and soul. A clarion call eliciting an instant clamouring acceptance from his body, even though his mind teetered on a refusal.

"Stay."

Thea kissed him again. A deeper, more carnal kiss than the first.

"Stay Josh," she repeated. "You know you want to." She rubbed her lithe body against his traitorous erection, letting him know she was aware of his desire.

"Are you sure?"

Although his every instinct was to rush her to the nearest bedroom, he felt obliged to offer her a chance to change her mind.

Thea vaguely recalled vowing to back off and let Josh set the pace. That was then. Now, the situation was something else entirely. She leaned heavily against him, forcing him to support her weight with his hands.

"Positive. I don't want to be alone tonight." She thought a moment, remembering how loyalty to his dead wife had caused him to back off once before.

"I know your heart belongs to Ellie, and always will," she murmured, looking him squarely in the eye.

"But Josh, she has no use for your body; and I do."

Thea was surprised at how free she felt, knowing this. Free to enjoy herself with no danger of hurting him. No danger of being hurt, since she knew the score and wasn't looking for Forever.

After all the walking on eggshells with Dot, afraid of doing harm through some careless word or action, it felt wonderful to simply blurt out what she wanted. She smiled radiantly up at Josh, willing him to agree.

She's right. Go for it.

It was Ellie's voice in Josh's mind.

Again.

Saying what he wanted to hear.

At first, hearing her in his mind had made Ellie feel close to him; almost as if she'd never left him. But, a sceptic in matters of the paranormal, he'd suspected for some time it was really his own subconscious self, using her beloved voice to persuade him to do what was right.

Or what he really wanted to do.

But whichever of them had spoken, Josh now realised it was time to be moving on.

Time to begin living again.

Last night he'd been scheming for just this opportunity, only to be denied by circumstances.

Not tonight. Josh wrapped both arms around Thea, returning her kisses; with interest.

His hands ranged over and around Thea, learning the shape of her body. They threaded themselves through her hair, learning its silky texture. And his mouth devoured her.

Thea followed Josh's lead, her body tingling with the friction of his roving hands. Leaning back, she slipped her hands between them to work on his buttons.

Immediately he returned the favour. Extended it, delving eagerly beneath the folds of shirt and jacket to cup his hands around breasts already swollen and heavy.

Thea shivered. Baring his chest in turn, she purred deep in her throat, her hands grazing over broad pectoral muscles with their dusting of soft, dark hair. Leaning in, she laid a trail of biting kisses from one flat, brown nipple to the other, pausing there to suckle before trailing back to the other side.

Josh shuddered. Groaned his pleasure. But being on the receiving end wasn't enough.

He wanted, needed, to bestow pleasure equally. Bending his head, he took one tight, rosy bud into his mouth, boosting her to a comfortable height with his hands caught under her thighs.

Nothing loath, Thea wrapped both legs around his waist, clinging with one arm round his shoulders, her free hand rubbing teasing little circles over the fascinating masculine chest which still held her in thrall. Leaning back, she gave him maximum access to her throbbing breasts.

Access he was only to happy to take advantage of. Feeling the edge of the table behind him, Josh swung his precious burden around, dropping her lightly onto the tabletop to give himself the unfettered use of both hands.

"Owww!" Thea wailed, promptly jumping down to the floor. "Mr Prickles!" Swallowing an indignant laugh, she rubbed her injured posterior.

"You dumped me right on top of him," she accused. "Poor little beast."

"Never mind him. He's built to take it. Let me see if you're hurt, Thea." Suiting actions to words, Josh boldly unzipped her jeans, pushing them low enough to see the rash of red dots across her bottom.

"Not too bad," he pronounced.

"I take it that's an expert medical opinion?" Thea sounded faintly aggrieved, but her smile belied the hint of annoyance.

Josh grinned.

"As expert as needed. Here, let me kiss it better."

"I feel absolutely certain it's going to take an awful lot of kissing to cure being spiked by a robo-echidna." Hauling her jeans up with one hand to keep from tripping over them, Thea held out the other to take Josh by the hand.

"Let's move the surgery into the bedroom to avoid a second attack."

Undressing each other, and the kissing better of Thea's wounds entailed gales of laughter and much physical contact. Which rapidly led to arousing caresses of a more intimate nature.

Thea had never felt so comfortable with a lover. So free of all those niggling doubts and worries that caused her to hold back; to keep a part of herself separate from the action.

Laughter and joking had never been part of lovemaking before, but with Josh they were. With Josh Marten she felt completely free and easy.

She simply *knew* they'd be perfect together.

And we were, she thought sleepily a considerable time later.

Sprawled bonelessly across his torso, she heard his heart beating beneath her ear. Felt it too. The steady lub-dub-dub vibrated through her body, her own resting heartbeat resonating in unison with it.

Coming more awake by the minute, she made an interesting discovery. One that roused the devil in her.

He's still inside me!

Sometime after Josh had brought them both to a wonderful, earth-moving orgasm, he'd carefully rolled over without disengaging to bring her on top. "Don't want to crush you, Thea," he'd murmured, sinking into well-earned slumber.

Loving the replete feeling of their intimate connection, Thea also drowsed off. Now she was awake, and he was still inside her.

Smiling to herself, Thea used her inner muscles to caress him. His heartbeat jumped. Her smile deepening, she caressed him again. This time there was an answering twitch, and the swelling feel of the beast returning to life, filling her to repletion once again.

"Damn it, Woman," the stirring male beneath her rasped. "Can't a man get any sleep around here? You're an insatiable wench, you are, Thea Benson."

On the words, he reached up to clasp her face, drawing her to him for another of his shattering kisses. By the time he released her mouth, he was moving rhythmically within her. Rising onto her knees, Thea matched him, stroke for stroke.

"Seems you're pretty insatiable yourself, Lover-boy. I do like a man with stamina. I was afraid you were going to waste the night sleeping."

"That's enough cheek from you." He swatted her lightly on the rump.

Thea giggled, and stepped the pace up a notch, until she rode him hell-for-leather into a starry oblivion. He shouted her name when he came, and as she sank into darkness, she heard her own scream echoing in her head.

~~~~~

In her dream her lover stroked a hand slowly down her thigh, his hand returning to slip, featherlight, across her tummy.

"Mmmm."

Her dream lover eased his magical hand higher, cupping one heavy breast. His breath whispered across the back of her neck as his lips caressed her. Thea stretched voluptuously, willing the dream to continue. She could feel him stretched out behind her, spooning her against his aroused body.

Her dream lover kneaded her breast, and nipped her shoulder, ruthlessly dragging her out of the dream. To the realisation she was not alone. Thea stiffened. Then relaxed as memory flooded back. Josh Marten. Not a dream, then. He'd stayed the night. She cracked her eyes open a fraction, squinting at the bright morning light.

Another nip.

The hand at her breast tugged at the nipple, demanding her attention. In case she hadn't got the message yet, Josh moved against her, his rock-hard erection prodding her back, making his intentions unmistakeable.

Thea yawned, rolling to face him, wrapping her arms around his neck. It was a long time since she'd last woken to discover a man in her bed. Reality was so much better than a dream.

Indulging herself, she kissed him. A long, languid kiss with lots of tongue. Recalling how he'd nipped her into wakefulness, she ended with a payback nip to his bottom lip, then soothed the hurt with another kiss.

"At last," her partner growled. "I thought you'd never wake up. You sleep like the dead, Thea Benson."

He accompanied his words by sliding one long finger inside her, withdrawing it to tease the sensitive nub at her entrance.

"Now who's being insatiable?"

More than willing, Thea accidently caught a glimpse of her bedside clock, and gasped. Almost eight! In all the excitement the night before she'd forgotten to set the alarm. She pushed herself upright, tossing the covers back.

"Sorry Lover-boy. Some of us work to a timetable and can't laze around half the day. Out you get!"

"I can be quick. I'll even make breakfast for you while you shower."

Thea reconsidered.

"Sounds a good deal. How quick is quick?"

Letting his actions speak for themselves, Josh pulled her back into the bed. Flipping her onto her back, he was inside her so fast she squealed.

Clutching his shoulders, Thea wrapped her legs around him and laughing, held on for the ride. A hard, fast ride ending with a glorious starburst. She'd barely caught her breath when Josh ruthlessly hauled her onto her feet.

"Quick enough?"

Thea laughed again, and moved in for another kiss.

"No time for that."

He swatted her lightly across her backside and turned her in the direction of her bathroom. "You've got a timetable to keep to, remember?"

Thea laughed again.

14

Fifteen minutes later, dressed in her tunic and leggings for work, Thea entered her kitchen, not sure what to expect.

"I'm starving. Breakfast better be good."

"Every bit as good as you were last night."

A towel tucked in the waistband of his jeans, Josh whisked her chair out and seated her at the table.

"And this morning," he added, placing a mug of freshly brewed coffee in front of her. A bowl of muesli, yogurt and fresh berries already awaited her.

"Yumm," Thea hummed her approval. "Although I reckon it should be 'as good as *we* were', you know. There were two of us in that bed, and I didn't notice either one of us shirking. I had the best time, Josh."

Eyes on her plate, her cheeks warm and rosy, she tucked into her breakfast.

"You're right. And the good time was mutual. You're a good sport, Thea Benson."

Not quite the accolade she'd expected to hear Not precisely words to make her hum with pleasure, they dimmed Thea's post-coital euphoria. She'd had more than a mere 'good time'. She waited to hear him say something more personal.

Something along the lines of "You're such a fantastic lover I can't wait to make love to you again."

A one-night stand certainly wasn't enough for her! She waited a second, but Josh seemed to have said all he was going to.

Containing her disappointment, Thea scooped up another spoonful and changed the subject.

"How did you know this is what I like for breakfast?"

"I looked in the fridge, didn't I. There's muffins with bacon and eggs when you finish that."

The toaster popped, and Josh turned back to his culinary tasks while Thea finished her cereal. At least the breakfast satisfied her expectations.

"So. Thea. What have you got lined up for today?" Josh delivered the promised bacon and eggs along with his rather diffident question.

"The usual round of appointments, although I'm expecting a lot of nosey questions. Eddie, Dot and Sophie were gearing up for a round of 'confidential' phone calls to people they 'know they can trust' when I left them yesterday afternoon. People they know they can trust to spread a juicy bit of news to all and sundry, is how I read it." She paused to devour a morsel of perfectly cooked egg. Swallowing, she continued. "Tonight, I'm having dinner with Dot and Sophie."

She sat lost in thought for a long moment, considering her words. Looking directly at her companion, she dazzled him with a radiant smile.

"I'm having dinner *with my mother and my sister!*"

She dabbed at her eyes with a tissue.

"Oh Josh, you've no idea how absolutely amazing it feels to say that. I thought it was something which could never happen, and now it has, it gives me a tingly feeling all over."

"I've got a pretty good imagination." His voice gruff, Josh continued. "I'm happy for you, Thea. You deserve a bit of happiness."

Between Ellie and his mother, Josh had picked up good kitchen habits, Thea mused a while later. Breakfast had continued with only the most banal of conversation, and now, while she finished loading the dishwasher, Josh dealt with those items requiring a hand wash.

Draining the last mouthful of her coffee, she bent to put the mug on its tray. A hand on her arm had her straightening to look over her shoulder.

"I'm off now, Thea. Don't want to get caught leaving and expose you to even more gossip. Before I go, though I …" He ran a hand through his mane, rumpling its freshly-combed neatness.

Thea studied him, eyebrow raised in silent interrogation.

"The thing is," he said, the words tumbling over themselves, "I want to see you again. Only I don't know when. Or if you even want to?"

Thea nodded.

She wanted to alright.

Did she ever.

This was what she'd wanted to hear earlier. She smiled, encouraging him to go on.

"You've got family tonight, and I've got fire brigade tomorrow."

Thea nodded again. She knew he'd joined the local volunteer brigade soon after arriving in The Crossing. The only regular community interaction he'd had until recently, she assumed he had been motivated by his feelings over Ellie's death in a house fire.

"We're doing a hazard-reduction burn, so we'll be late. Maybe Wednesday? Or Thursday? …" His words trailed off inconclusively.

"Let's say Wednesday," Thea took pity on him, "but leave it open to negotiation if either of us discovers they have something on."

"Sounds like a plan. Bye. And … Thanks, Thea."

He hauled her up against him for a kiss which left her in no doubt his future plans included a whole lot more than sharing a glass of wine.

Then he was gone, leaving her looking after him, a goofy smile on her face.

I'm so lucky, she told herself.

I've discovered a mother who really wants me, and I'm getting great sex with no tricky strings to get tangled up in.

Hearing a car pull up out front, Thea closed the dishwasher and went through to let in Vera Nicols and Lisa Tan, the stylist and apprentice she'd inherited from Toni Molloy.

~~~~~

"Thea! Thea! Is it true? Is Dot James really your mother? Only Hazel Whitman told Mum, and she'd know, wouldn't she? Being Sophie's mother-in-law and Dot's best friend."

Lisa's excited babble of questions set the tone for the day - for the rest of the week, in fact – as Thea had expected. By the time she had run through the agreed-upon spiel for the umpteenth dozen time, she felt comfortable in her new role of Dot's long-lost daughter.

Arriving on Dot's doorstep that evening, wine and chocolates in hand, pleasurable excitement fizzed through her veins.

Thea would never have believed what a difference it made, being part of a family. Sharing hugs and kisses with Dot and Sophie, knowing it was her mother and sister she hugged and kissed, was far more special than sharing similar greetings with even her very best friends. She felt like laughing and crying all at once.

This was a relationship she'd treasure, and carefully nurture for as long as she lived.

Even her growing feelings for Josh Marten paled in comparison.

Happily accepting a glass of wine, she sat down in what had rapidly become 'her' chair, feeling this was as good as it got, only to be forced to instantly revise her estimation.

Thea set her glass down as Dot leant towards her, claiming both her hands in a firm grip.

"I don't know how you feel about it, Thea Darling," Dot said, nerves rendering her voice squeaky and breathless, "but do you think you could bring yourself to call me 'Mum'?"

Tears flooded Thea's eyes, just when she'd thought she had no more left to shed.

"I'll understand if it's too soon," Dot said, the words tumbling over themselves they came out in such a rush, her radiant joy dimming as she spoke, "but, please, Darling, will you think about it?"

"Oh! Oh," Thea gasped.

"No need to think. Mum," she added, blushing through her tears as she tried out the simple little syllable. "It's how I've begun thinking of you in my mind. Only, ..." She turned agonised eyes towards her sister.

"What about Sophie?"

Oh, she thought, *I don't think I could bear it if Sophie doesn't like it.*

"Silly."

Sophie came and perched on the arm of Thea's chair, slinging an arm around her shoulders and squeezing hard. "Mum and I talked before you arrived. I've always wanted a sister, and now I've got one. I know Mum loves me, and you know, Thea? The more love you give, the more you have to share. It's one of life's wonderful mysteries; so, you see, you needn't worry about taking what's mine. Mum's got love enough for both of us."

By the time Sophie finished speaking, all three women were wiping their eyes.

~~~~~

It was quite late when Josh saw Thea saying goodnight to Sophie outside her gate. He hadn't been waiting up for her.

Not exactly.

He told himself he'd wanted to be sure the evening had gone well for Thea. From the sounds of laughter and cheerful farewells carrying clearly on the still night air, he felt safe in assuming it had.

Sitting in the dark on his veranda, watching Sophie disappear from sight into her house, he was tempted to go to Thea. Following their night together, he didn't think she'd turn him away, but it was very late. Unlike him, she couldn't lie in in the morning.

Besides, he didn't want her thinking he was some ravening beast, even though he was rock-hard every time he thought of her. Something he'd done far too often today. No, he reckoned he'd exercise a bit of self-control and wait till Wednesday as they'd agreed.

He tossed back the last of his whiskey and turned in.

15

In the middle of touching up the grey in Barbara Morgan's smooth, brown crop, late Wednesday afternoon, Thea suddenly realised she had no idea what her date with Josh entailed. Or even if it could rightly be termed a date.

It had hurriedly been agreed they'd see each other on Wednesday. Time, location and whether or not a meal was part of the arrangement hadn't been mentioned. And she hadn't seen hide nor hair of that annoying man next door since. Not so much as a fleeting glimpse.

For all she knew, he could have gone away.

Taking a quick coffee break between appointments, she flicked through the phone book, only to discover Josh Marten wasn't listed.

Of course he wasn't, misanthropic hermit that he was. There went Plan A. *It's probably to the good,* she consoled herself. *I don't want to appear to be hounding the man.*

She was turning over a variety of options for Plan B when Lisa Tan called her name, waving the phone in the air.

"Thea Benson speaking," she uttered in crisp, businesslike tones. Hearing the voice of the man who'd been occupying her thoughts for the last half hour, her heart did a quick double beat then settled back into its regular rhythm.

Is he psychic, or is it just a coincidence?

"Do you want to make an appointment?"

Aware of the salon full of sharp ears with nothing better to do than listen in to her conversation, Thea carefully maintained a bland expression and forbore to call Josh by name. Somehow, she didn't think he'd welcome being the subject of the next story on the bush telegraph.

"An appointment? Well, that's one way of putting it I guess," he teased, amazing Thea with his playfulness when she was more accustomed to terse growls. "Let's say my place. Six o'clock. I'm cooking." That sounded more like him, Thea thought.

"Okay."

"Nosy parkers in earshot?"

"That's right."

"See you at six." With that, he hung up.

Doing likewise, Thea went through the motions of making a fictious entry in the appointments book, mentally reminding herself to erase it later.

~~~~~

On Wednesday night Thea and Josh, to their mutual satisfaction, christened the well-sprung king-sized bed Josh had taken delivery of the week before.

Thursday night was more of the same. Friday though, …

"Can't. I'm going to the pub for dinner," Thea told him when he asked. "Mum … Oh my God, Josh. I still go tingly all over when I say it. Mum wants a public showing. Should be quite a crowd."

Glancing sidelong at him, she offered a counter suggestion to the one he'd just made.

"Why don't you come along with me?" At his look of horror, she had to sit down, she laughed so hard.

"Why not, Josh?" she teased, swallowing the last of her giggles.

"It's inevitable the old tabbies will find out about us sooner or later. There's nothing wrong with being friends with benefits, you know, as long as *we're* both comfortable with the arrangement."

"Friends with benefits? That how you see us, Thea? Just a comfortable arrangement?"

What's he scowling about?

All of a sudden, the conversation was full of booby-traps.

"Well, isn't it?" she challenged. "There's never been any suggestion it's otherwise. We're both enjoying a healthy case of mutual lust."

And that's all it is, she reminded herself. *I'd be a fool to expect more from a man who's still in love with his dead wife.*

Josh looked as if he had a sour taste in his mouth.

Shoving his hands in the back pockets of his jeans he stood looking out the window.

Just when Thea was about to give up on an answer, he straightened, moving his hands to his hips and looking her in the face.

"I don't like the idea of you being subjected to more gossip on top of all the rest with Dot. It's not fair to you, and she probably wouldn't like it either."

Thea nodded cautiously. He was likely right. Dorothy James was rather more straight-laced than most.

"So, no, Thea. I won't be going to the pub with you. Friends is fine in public, but I'll thank you to keep our 'arrangement', as you term it, between the two of us."

"Sure, Josh. Gotta run."

Thea kissed him in a manner guaranteed to stir his baser instincts, then jogged out and back across to her cottage. If they were careful, she reckoned they could probably stay under the radar till their affair burnt itself out.

~~~~~

Caught up in a whirlwind of hugs, kisses and congratulations from the Friday evening crowd, it was some time before Dot, Sophie and Thea took their places at their table. Dot, beaming with pleasure, looked from one young woman to the other.

"Goodness," she exclaimed softly. "With all your fancy hair colours, Thea, I hadn't realised how much alike you two girls are. Now that you've gone back to your natural brown, there's no mistaking you're sisters."

"It's actually a relief to be my normal self again," Thea replied. "I was getting rather tired of being in disguise."

"Well I think it's lovely having a big sister," Sophie chipped in. "I always wanted one. Look, someone's given us a bottle of bubbly. The good stuff, too," she added, pulling the chilled bottle out of the ice bucket to examine the label.

Reading the card tied around the neck, she murmured, "I wonder who? It just says to Dorothy James and her daughters."

Phil Morris wandered up from where he'd been watching, overhearing Sophie's words.

"Good evening, ladies. The champers is courtesy of Josh Marten. He came in earlier today and ordered it. Since he's the thorn between you two lovely roses, Sophie and Thea, residentially speaking of course, he reckoned he owed you a congratulatory tipple."

The gesture gave Thea a warm feeling. For an antisocial curmudgeon, Josh was sometimes surprisingly sweet.

"Shall I do the honours for you?"

Receiving Dot's assent, Phil deftly opened the bottle and filled their glasses.

Looking up as they clinked glasses in a toast, Dot spotted their benefactor entering the dining room.

"Josh!" she called.

Jumping up, she ran over to thank him for his generous gift, bringing him over to the table with her for the girls to add their thanks to hers.

"Why don't you join us?" Sophie asked, bolder than Thea dared to be.

"Can't, ladies. I'm meeting Len and Mili. Enjoy yourselves."

With that, he crossed to the other side of the room where the Woodcocks were perusing the menu.

A couple of hours later, when Thea left with Sophie, it appeared a coincidence when Josh fell into step beside them. A carefully orchestrated coincidence, Thea felt. An assumption he confirmed when he eased out of the shadows on her patio after she'd called a last goodnight to Sophie as she entered her house on the other side of his.

"For a man trying to avoid gossip, you take extraordinary risks," she commented. "Champagne, and then walking me home."

"Calculated risks. And it wasn't exclusively you. Anyway, I've got better things to talk about." He pulled her close, sealing her lips with a kiss before she could utter another word.

16

It was almost two weeks later when the afternoon peace was shattered by the wailing of a loud siren, making everyone in the salon jump and clap their hands to their ears.

"Omigod, that's the fire siren." Lisa Tan's words were shouted above the noise. "Gotta go, Thea."

She turned the water off where she was washing Mili Woodcock's hair prior to her regular perm. Stripping off her pinafore, she grabbed her bag and ran for the door.

"What ...?"

"She's a fire brigade volunteer," Vera reminded Thea. "The siren alerts town members they're needed. Quicker than the phone, since half of them don't carry their phones in their back pockets all the time. Wonder where the fire is?"

Looking down the street after Lisa, Thea noticed Josh's battered ute stop to give her a lift. Another volunteer answering the call to duty. The klaxon blare of the siren had stopped, leaving a tense silence behind it. Shortly after, the first of the town's two fire tankers roared past, lights flashing.

As Thea hastened to cover for Lisa's absence, she gave silent thanks for a slack afternoon. Looking around, she noticed the couple of ladies who'd been idly chatting earlier were now working their phones.

"House fire out at Granny Elliot's place." Bea Anderson was first with her triumphant announcement. "They'll never save that dump. It's a tinderbox waiting for a match. Wonder what set it off?"

"Hope the old lady got out safely," Vera said, reminding them all that fires threatened lives as well as property.

Stay safe, Josh, Thea prayed silently, her stomach clenching in fear.

It wasn't long before Sergeant Don Matthews roared past, closely followed by the second fire truck, manned by a crew from nearby farms who necessarily took longer to report for duty. An unusual number of cars and utes were also speeding out of town, all heading towards the fire.

Thea and Vera worked steadily, trying to ignore the hyped-up atmosphere. They'd whittled the queue down to Mili and Bea when another siren and flashing lights speeding by had them all turning to the plate-glass front window which gave such an excellent view of the road outside.

"Ambulance." Mili stated the obvious.

"Wonder who they've been called for?" Bea was agog with curiosity. "Maybe the old lady got caught when that old wooden shack of hers went up. She's just down the track from my place. Hurry up and finish my hair, Thea. I want to get out there before it's all over."

Ghoul! Thea thought, but she obligingly applied herself to getting Bea on her way in the shortest possible time.

By the time Mili left, patting her freshly permed waves, the ambulance and one of the fire trucks had returned, both entering town at a sedate observance of the speed limit, unlike on their departure.

"Not too serious, then," Vera observed.

"Unless they were too late to save her," Mili chipped in. "There'd be no need to rush in that case."

An observation which did nothing to ease the anxious roiling in Thea's gut.

What if it was one of the firefighters? She had more friends among them than Josh and Lisa.

It was a relief to shut the door behind Vera when they'd finished cleaning up at the end of the afternoon. Reluctant to move out of sight of the traffic, not that she could do anything, Thea sat down to catch up on paperwork.

Jumping nervously when the phone rang, she picked it up, a horrible premonition of bad news making it difficult to answer calmly.

"Thea Benson?"

"That's right. How may I help you?"

"Matron Porteus here. From the hospital. One of our patients asked me to call you. Josh Marten. Says you're his next-door neighbour."

"Yes. Yes … Matron, how bad is he? It's just that he went out to the fire earlier and I've been worrying."

"Well you can stop worrying right this minute. He's just got a bit of smoke inhalation. Will be right as rain in a couple of days. That young man's a hero, you know." It seemed Matron was inclined to chat, so Thea made an encouraging noise and listened carefully.

"As I heard it, the brigade had just arrived to find Danny Anderson and Mrs Elliot doing their best with a garden hose, when the old lady gave a shriek and ran back into the house. Saw her cat scratching frantically at the window, Danny said. Our Mr Marten grabbed a fire blanket and dashed in after her." Matron slowed for a breath, then took up the tale again.

"The rest of the crew trained their hoses around the front door until Mr Marten staggered out with her wrapped in the fireproof blanket. He even had the dratted cat stuffed down his jacket," she laughed.

"So they're both alright?" Thea, relieved, wasn't quite ready to relax.

"Just a bit of smoke inhalation, like I said, and a smattering of fairly mild burns. We're keeping both of them in for a bit in case there's any adverse reactions. Which brings me to the reason I'm calling you, Thea. Josh wants you to pop over to his house, says you know where the key is, and pack a bag for him. PJs, toiletries and a clean outfit to wear home tomorrow or the next day."

"Okay, Matron. I'll be there shortly. Thanks for relieving my mind. I was really worried. No other firefighters hurt?"

"No. But apparently the house is a total write-off. Bye." Hanging up, Thea wiped a tear from her eye, noticing for the first time that her hands were trembling.

She picked up her coffee, using both hands to hold it steady, and took a long swallow. By the time her mug was empty, the trembling fit was over and she was beginning to feel a bit brighter.

~~~~~

The racket could be heard from the street outside the small cottage hospital.

"Sounds like you've got half The Crossing up here, Matron."

Fran Porteus shrugged lightly.

"You're right there, Thea. The men's ward is overflowing with firefighters. They came straight here. Still in their filthy gear, stinking the whole place up with the smell of smoke and dropping clots of dirt off their boots on my nice, clean floors. I only let them in because I reckoned it might help settle their nerves. It shook some of them up pretty badly to see one of their own come so close to being burnt alive. It's every firefighter's worst nightmare, you know."

She smoothed the old-fashioned crisp, white uniform, tucked a stray lock of hair behind her ear, and set off down the hallway.

"Time to turf the lot of them out and get this place back to normal. You can take that bag in when the room's clear."

"Time, gentlemen. On your way now. Let the lad get some rest."

Nurses! Thea smiled to herself listening to Matron laying down the law in the time-honoured authoritarian manner of her profession.

Everyone grumbled about their bossiness; until they found themselves in need of a bit of care, then the women were hailed as angels of mercy.

"Yeah, yeah Franny Love. We're just leaving."

"See ya round Marten."

"You're a bloody hero, Mate. You deserve a medal for what you did out there today."

The first of Josh's visitors were spilling out the door into the corridor when a burly bloke Thea had seen around town a few times eased through the front door, making a beeline for the men's ward. She followed him in time to see him dodge around Fran Porteus and reach out to vigorously shake Josh's hand.

"Danny Elliot. Thanks for saving the Old Girl, Mate. She's a stubborn old cow, but she's me Mum, so what can I say? Would've hated to see her end up burnt to a crisp." He shook Josh's hand again.

"As for that blasted cat," he continued," the mangy animal oughta be put down, so it should; only the Old Girl dotes on it, so I've dropped it off at the vet's. Probably gunna cost me an arm and a leg before it's done. Thanks again Mate. I'll just be off now to see how Mum's doin'."

"Thea. Sorry to let you down this arvo." Following her male colleagues, Lisa Tan, a diminutive figure in her yellow overalls, stopped to give Thea a hug.

"Don't be silly, Lisa. What you did was way more important than Mili Woodcock's perm. Are you sure you're okay?" She held the girl at arm's length, examining her carefully for signs of damage.

Receiving a nod, she bit back the words trembling on the tip of her tongue. In her opinion, the girl looked on the verge of tears, but she didn't want to embarrass her in front of the men. She'd already had a tough struggle to be accepted as an equal in the brigade.

"Take some time off if you need it," she murmured, hugging Lisa back.

By that time the room had emptied out and Fran Porteus was ushering her in.

"Here Thea is with the things you asked for, Josh. Ten minutes, Thea, then he really does need to rest."

"Will do."

Thea quietly shut the door behind the Matron. Turning, she got her first clear view of Josh.

"Josh! Oh God, Josh," she gasped.

"They told me you were alright. Just a bit of smoke inhalation, but you've been burnt." She reached out a tentative hand to stroke his close-cropped head and chin. Without his long hair and thick beard, he didn't look like the Josh Marten she knew. Trying not to stare, she studied the shape of his head, finding him distinctly handsome, even allowing for the effects of the fire.

"I'm okay," he rasped. "Hair caught alight on the way out. Turned the hose on me, so only a bit of hair missing. Gimme a kiss, Woman"

Gingerly, she complied, noting his hiss of pain when she made contact with his damaged lips. More than hair had suffered during his heroic rescue exploit.

Drawing back, she catalogued a number of small burns on his face and neck, but since none appeared major injuries, she contented herself with a single comment.

"Idiot," she said, laying her hand affectionately on his good cheek, lips curving into a shaky smile, "Just had to play hero, didn't you?"

He turned his head to kiss her palm just as the '1812 Overture' sounded from the bag she was still holding.

"You answer," he mouthed.

"Josh Marten's phone."

"Where's my Josh? Who are you? Let me talk to Josh."

"Mum," Josh croaked, taking the phone back and holding it close to his mouth. "Calm down, Mum. I'm okay." His words did little to stem the noisy sobs echoing round the room.

"Throat hurts. You talk to her, Thea." She nodded, sitting close to Josh on the edge of the bed.

"Mrs Marten, listen to me." She spoke as firmly as she could. "Mrs Marten, Josh is right here, listening. He's okay. Truly." The sobs abated.

"Are you sure?"

"Very sure, Mrs Marten. He's in hospital because he breathed in a bit too much smoke. His throat's sore, and he's a bit short of breath, but he'll be alright in a few days. You can stop worrying."

For the next few moments there was silence, except for a choked-back sniffle down the line, and Josh's raspy breathing.

"Are you a nurse?"

"No, Mrs Marten. I'm Thea Benson, Josh's neighbour."

"Oh. I want to talk to my son, Ms Benson. Put him on, please."

"Certainly, Mrs Marten. I'll leave the two of you alone to talk in private, but remember, his throat hurts and he's finding it hard to talk." Thea handed the phone to Josh and turned to go.

"Don't leave," he whispered, then addressed himself to his mother. "Mum."

Thea compromised by walking out of the room, but remaining within sight. Just as well, since she'd hardly taken up her position before Josh was beckoning madly, a hunted expression on his face. He thrust the phone into her hand, then leaned back against his pillows looking utterly exhausted.

Cautiously, she gripped the phone, switching it to speaker to share with Josh.

"Mrs Marten!" The woman was sobbing again and she had to speak quite loudly to make herself heard.

"Oh. You're back." The lack of enthusiasm made Thea cringe internally. "You said my son's alright, but he can barely speak, and I saw the utube video a little while ago. He was coming out of a burning house, and *he was on fire*! I saw it. How can he be alright? You're lying to me!"

What utube video?

Realising she had little hope of convincing Josh's mother she was speaking the truth, she hurried to find Fran Porteus. Maybe the Matron would have the authority to calm her fears.

As soon as she was free, she searched her phone, easily finding the video. No wonder his mother was upset. Especially since she'd already lost Josh's wife, Ellie, in a house fire. Thea felt ashamed of her impatience.

Shortly after, she left Josh to rest, promising to return the next day. She grinned, seeing Matron switch his phone off and stow it in the bedside locker, out of sight.

17

"They're cutting me loose."

"Oh, thank God."

After watching the video being played over and over on the television news, Thea had more sympathy with Josh's mother than she'd had when they spoke. Some bystander had photographed the rescue on their phone and uploaded it to the local television network.

The flames blooming momentarily around Josh's face as he emerged from the blazing house, the old lady wrapped in a silver fire blanket in his arms, looked so much scarier on the big screen. Even though she knew the truth, Thea had had a hard time believing Josh truly wasn't badly burnt. How much worse it must have been for his mother!

"Pick me up, Thea?"

"Sure. Tell me when."

In the event, when she took an early break and went to fetch him, she found him being lectured by Matron Porteus.

"You're not one hundred percent recovered yet, you know, Josh. When you get home, you take it easy and rest," she ordered. "You heard what Doc Roberts told you. No work. Especially not your kind of work, until your airways are completely clear."

Snickering a little, Thea stepped forward. "Leave him to me, Matron," she said, ignoring Josh's exaggerated eye roll behind Matron's back. "If he steps out of line, I'll get Eddie Patterson to organise a roster of nursemaids to watch him."

"She'd do it, too, if I know Eddie," Matron chuckled.

Josh huffed a little as both women laughed, but pinned by Matron's rapidly assumed steely glare, he acquiesced. Surreptitiously, Thea checked him out, happy to note how much better he looked after a night's rest. The burns weren't quite as red, and were scabbing over already.

"C'mon Mate," she urged, beating him to pick up his bag. "I've got a business to run. Let's get you settled so I can get back to my clients."

~~~~~

Although Thea had popped across a couple of times during the afternoon, it wasn't till she arrived at dusk with a pot of lamb stew and all the trimmings, that there was time for them to talk. Really talk, about what had happened the day before.

"How come it was you who went in after her, Josh? You're still a trainee, aren't you?"

"Yeah, but ..." Josh trailed away into silence, remembering his captain whispering in his ear about them having a talk when he was up to it.

He'd broken the rules. Rules that existed to protect the firefighters as well as the public. He knew more lives than his and old Mrs Elliot's had been on the line yesterday.

If he hadn't got out when he did, someone else would have been sent to rescue *him*.

"I wasn't doing anything else at the time. The fire blanket was there, next to me, and I saw her dash for the door before the others did." Trying to recall the sequence of events accurately, he frowned.

"Thing was, Thea, I just acted without thinking. I'm lucky the others on my team were on the ball, aiming the hoses to keep the doorway clear as long as they did, or it might all have ended differently." He shuddered involuntarily.

"Well, however it happened, you're the hero of the hour, Josh. I'm so proud of you." She leaned over to kiss him gently, careful of his burnt lips. When he pulled back, shaking his head, she stared at him, confused.

"Not a hero. I feel such a hypocrite every time someone says that."

"How would you put it then?"

"Stupid fool. Worse even. Bart Gibson is just waiting to get me on my own to tear a strip off me."

"He's brigade captain, isn't he?"

"Yeah. He's right, Thea. I didn't think."

He stared into space, plucking up the courage to tell Thea the truth.

Will she ever trust me again if I do?

The thought of losing her gnawed at him, but if he didn't give her the truth, he'd never be comfortable round her again. Turning away, he stared out at nothing, and let the words flow.

"The fire seduced me, Thea. All I could see was Ellie. Burning. And me not there to save her. As I ran in after Mrs Elliot, it was Ellie I was rescuing. Then I remembered she was dead. The thought crossed my mind that I could let the fire take me. Join her."

He felt Thea's hand clasp his, and glanced down at their joined hands, relief flooding over him.

"You didn't though."

Her words, almost too soft to be heard, prompted him to finish the story.

"No. I'd jumped in, so it was up to me to get the old lady out, or others would have to come after both of us, and there'd be the risk of a major catastrophe."

He stalled again. Gripping Thea's hand tightly, he drew strength from her.

"Something else. I suddenly realised I didn't want to die. Even if it meant being reunited with Ellie forever. I wanted to live. After her, … I prayed to die back then. When it didn't happen, I gradually started making a new life for myself. Was making a bloody mess of it till you came along, with your pink hair and spying on people." He squeezed Thea's hand and slanted a lop-sided grin in her direction.

"You started me looking outside myself. Yesterday, I knew I wanted to live. So I could come back to you. I realised Ellie is my past. You're my future, Thea."

He waited, but Thea didn't speak, so he continued his story.

"So," he rasped. "I wrapped the fire blanket around the old lady and the stuffed the bloody cat she cared so much about down my overalls, and got the hell out while I still could."

He looked at Thea, worrying himself sick when he saw she was frowning. She hadn't said a word. What was going through her mind?

He shook her hand, trying to jog her attention. He had more to say, but it looked as if she'd shut down on him. Finally, she stirred, coming back from whatever far place her thoughts had taken her, so he got on with it while he was on a roll.

"I didn't come up with all that right then. Just got the key points in a flash, you know, and sorted the rest out later, after Matron had tucked me in and it was quiet enough to think."

What's he mean? I'm his future?

Thea's blood had run cold hearing he'd been entertaining suicidal thoughts, however briefly. It shocked her to the core to know how close she'd come to losing him yesterday. No wonder she'd experienced such bad vibes when she saw him heading out to the fire.

But he hadn't given in. The fire hadn't seduced him. He'd resisted its lure. Her tension eased back a notch, and she mentally reviewed his words again.

What's he mean? I'm his future?

Her thoughts kept on wildly circling back to that statement.

Ellie being his past was a no brainer, but why was he claiming her, Thea, as the counter to Ellie? He loved Ellie.

No way he means he's switched to loving me!

Josh was the constant type.

The forever kind.

If she couldn't rely on him for that, then she didn't know him at all. It was too much to take in without warning. Determinedly, she pulled herself out of her introspection. Not ready yet to explore his thinking, she avoided the issue.

"You're still a hero, you know, even if it was accidental. I'm so glad you decided on life." She disengaged the hand he was holding. "I'm also happy if my antics helped you see you still have a life."

She rose to her feet and began collecting the dirty dishes.

"I'll put these in the dishwasher and make some coffee."

She didn't see Josh's shoulders slump, or the defeated expression on his face. Looked like he'd have to wait to tell her the rest of yesterday's revelation, and he didn't want to. It had been hard enough to get out as much as he had. Waiting to say the rest would make it all so much harder.

~~~~~

Back with the coffee, Thea kept up a steady patter of inconsequential small talk, regardless of Josh's lack of enthusiasm.

"Before I forget," she said, preparing to leave him to his own devices. "Did you call your mother? You said you were going to."

"Yeah," he assured her. "Mum was really freaking out yesterday. Being out of hospital has eased her mind a lot, although she's threatening to come and see for herself."

"I would too, if it was my son who nearly got burnt to death. She hasn't been to Oxley Crossing, has she? Bet she's really curious about what you're up to."

"Umm. I guess. I asked the family to give me some space, and they have. We're pretty close, and I know my withdrawal hurt them. I'd like to see them all, but not like this. I don't need to be nursed and fussed over. I had enough of that two years ago." He watched Thea, uncertain of her mood, then, desperate to learn his fate, decided to simply plunge in and take his chances.

"I thought it might be nicer to invite them all to come for our wedding."

"Wedding! What the Hell are you talking about? Seems the fire fried a few brain cells as well as singing your beard."

Thea backed away until she was halted by the wall at her back. Josh winced, but once started, doggedly persisted.

"I love you, Thea Benson. We're really good together. I reckon we oughta get married."

Thea looked at him, aghast.

"But … You can't be in love with me. It's Ellie who holds your heart. Even though she's gone."

Her failure to reciprocate his declaration of love didn't escape Josh's notice.

"Thea. You haven't been listening. While it's true Ellie will always live in my heart; she's my past. There's plenty of room in my heart for more. For you, because I love you too. You're my future, Thea. Will you please put me out of my misery and say you'll marry me?"

"I thought you were happy with us being friends-with-benefits. When did things change?"

"My body recognised I love you from the first time I saw you," he stated. "My heart and soul took a while longer to catch up. Yesterday's near-death experience clarified everything for me. Are you going to stand there pretending you don't love me? When we're together, we do more than have great sex, Thea. We make love with each other. Both of us. You can deny it all you want, but what we feel for each other is love."

He got up to stand in front of her, feet apart, arms crossed. A man in a dangerous mood.

Clutching her upper arms with both hands, Thea shuffled her feet, avoiding Josh's searching gaze.

"I'm not denying anything," she muttered. "So what if I love you? I like what we've got already. What if I agreed to marry you and it didn't work out? Where would that leave us?"

Couldn't the damned idiot see marriage wasn't necessary for them?

"I like what we've got, too, but don't you understand, Thea? It's not enough. I want so much more. I've been married. I know how much better we can be. I want us to live together. Share our lives. Have children. It all works better within marriage."

"You make it sound simple, Josh, but I know it's not." *Damn it all!* She brushed the moisture trickling down her cheek, determined not to cry. She was stronger than that.

"Lots of marriages start out with the couple madly in love only to end in a bitter divorce a few years later. How can you know that wouldn't happen to us?"

"You have a real problem with commitment, don't you, Thea?" Josh eased his aggressive stance, speaking gently.

His tenderness was nearly Thea's undoing. She sniffed back another incipient tear and tried not to look at him.

"It's the same as when you held back from telling Dot she was your mother. That's turned out really well, hasn't it?" Thea nodded slowly, but still looked unhappy.

"Trust in us, Thea," Josh urged, willing her to believe him. "We're not starry-eyed idiots thinking love will solve all problems. We both know relationships take work and commitment. We can do this if we both want it badly enough."

"You make it sound easy," she said again.

"And you're making it way harder than it needs to be."

"Yeah, well ... You've taken me by surprise. Can I have some time to think about it?"

"As long as you promise me you won't shut me out, you can have all the time you need." He wrapped both arms around her, drawing her in to his chest. Dropping a kiss on her forehead, he rocked her gently in his arms.

"I love you, Thea. And you love me. Be sure you don't lose sight of that while you're considering our future. Remember what good friends we are, and how good we are together."

"I will. Let me go, Josh. After all you've said, I need some time on my own. Goodnight."

Thea scuttled back to the sanctuary of her own house. Josh stood on his veranda, watching till long after her lights went out.

~~~~~

All Thea wanted was the oblivion of sleep. Sleep that remained stubbornly elusive.

What happened to being friends with benefits?

Why does Josh insist on wanting more?

More than I can give? Surely I'm not as dysfunctional as that!

But, … How do I know what's the right answer?

Every time she wound up asking herself the same question.

How do I know what's right for me?

If only there was someone she could turn to for advice.

But there is.

Thea sat straight up in her dishevelled bed and reached for the phone.

She supposed if she was her sister, Sophie, she'd be ringing her mother, she thought, scrolling through her contacts, only she didn't feel secure enough with Dot for such an intimate conversation. Maybe one day, but not yet. She slid her finger down to bring up the 'Ps', and pressed the button.

"Thea! Is something wrong?"

"No, Eddie. Not that kind of wrong."

She quite clearly heard Eddie Patterson's sigh of relief.

"Sorry to call so late and wake you. I'll be quick so you can get back to sleep. Eddie, when someone asks an important question, how do you know if the right answer is 'Yes' or 'No'?"

She couldn't be sure if the sound she heard was a cough or a smothered chuckle.

"It's not really all that tricky, Dear. I'll bet you're stewing over what might happen if you say 'Yes'? That offers too many options. Instead, try asking yourself how you'd feel if you said 'No'. If it makes you feel relieved, it's the right answer. If you feel you'll spend the rest of your life regretting the missed opportunity, then probably you should say 'Yes'. Does that help?"

"Not sure yet. I'm going to make some cocoa and sleep on it. Thanks, Eddie." Trust Eddie to hand the ultimate decision back to her. Looked like there was no easy way out for her.

Stirring the cocoa, Thea realised her mind was already throwing scenarios at her. Scenarios which all seemed to point her in one direction. Knowing she could always talk to Eddie again, at a more appropriate time, she thought this time she really would be able to sleep.

~~~~~

"Was that Thea Benson?" Mike Patterson yawned, glancing over at the bedside clock. Eddie nodded, carefully putting her phone down on her side of their bed.

"Doesn't she know what time it is?" he grumbled.

"Possibly not. She was in a bit of a state." Eddie settled down, pulling the covers up around her ears.

"I think I'll buy myself a new dress. A nice bold red, maybe. I predict we'll have another wedding to go to soon."

"Unless they do a runner like Alan and Angie, and elope," was the muffled comment from the other side of the bed.

18

Waking at her usual time, Thea bounced out of bed and hit the shower, mentally running through all the things she needed to accomplish before nine o'clock.

Top of the list was a visit to Josh Marten.

He'd asked her to marry him, and he deserved her answer as soon as she knew it. Which she now did.

Checking the time, she stepped into the kitchen and threw together the batter for a batch of waffles. Packing a bag with her waffle iron, a punnet of strawberries and a bottle of maple syrup and some cream, she added the bowl of batter and made a beeline for Josh's kitchen to finish cooking breakfast. Maybe if he was well fed, he'd forgive her her vacillations.

"Hang on," Josh shouted irritably. *Who the Hell was banging his door down at the crack of dawn?* Dragging on the jeans he'd tossed on the floor when he collapsed into bed the night before, he stumbled to the front door, flinging it open.

"What?" he half-shouted, scrabbling for a more conciliatory tone on seeing who stood there. "Sorry Thea. Come in."

"You look a bit rough. Sit down while I get the coffee on and cook some breakfast for you."

Breakfast! After the night he'd just had, Josh was tempted to tear a strip off her for waking him up what seemed mere minutes after he'd finally descended into sleep. Aided by his trusty bottle of Jameson's. Squinting against the light, he observed his tipple of choice had served him for the last time. He winced when Thea swept the empty bottle up and tossed it into the recycling bin with a noisy clatter.

He slumped at the table, watching morosely as she bustled around his kitchen.

"We need to talk."

In Josh's debilitated state, alarm bells rang. Her words sounded like a threat. No man in his right mind wanted to hear those words from his woman. Before breakfast. Which thought stirred his brain into sluggish gear.

He could think of only one topic Thea might want to discuss so urgently.

If she means to refuse me, why's she here at dawn, fixing breakfast? he mused. *Has to be a good bloody sign, hasn't it?*

Brightening somewhat, he roused himself even further when she slid a mug of steaming coffee in front of him. At least she seemed to have the priorities right.

While she cooked and set out plates, Thea maintained an inconsequential monologue which he'd studiously ignored. Now, fortified by caffeine, he felt up to contributing to the conversation.

"So, Thea, what's on your mind?"

"Last night you proposed. I'm here to accept."

"Just like that? Last night the very idea of marrying me had you freaking out. What's changed?"

Couldn't the damn man simply accept her answer without an inquisition? Apparently not. She eyed him glumly across the table.

"Nothing's changed. Not exactly. I told you last night I love you. I slept on it and decided I will marry you. Unless you've changed your mind."

Not bloody likely. She's accepted, and I'll hold her to it. Even if she does sound as if it's a fate worse than death.

"Then couldn't you at least try to sound a bit happier about it? Marrying me isn't a death sentence, you know. Nobody's forcing you." Her lack of her usual sparkling enthusiasm stung his ego, causing him to speak without thinking. That and his pounding headache courtesy of Mr Jameson.

"Keep that up and this may be the shortest engagement in history." Jumping to her feet, Thea began grabbing empty plates and tossing them into the sink to rinse them. Turning the water full on, she stumbled back when her carelessness resulted in a drenching.

"Now see what you've done!" She rounded on Josh, blaming him for her soaking.

About to answer back in similar vein, Josh was pulled up by Ellie's voice shouting in his mind to be heard above his mental clamour.

Do you want to marry her or not!

He did. He really did.

Time to think of her, then.

He carefully went to Thea. Wrapping his arms around her, he kissed her on the forehead and rocked her, making shushing noises.

A sniff told him how close his woman was to tears. He'd accused her of a lack of enthusiasm, but he'd been just as bloody-minded. Worse.

"We can do better than this, Love. I got to feeling sorry for myself last night and hit the bottle a bit hard. I shouldn't be taking my self-inflicted bad mood out on you. Let's start again, shall we?"

He swept her up in his arms and strode into the next room, sitting in his favourite armchair with Thea held firmly on his lap. He wasn't letting her go anywhere until she confirmed her acceptance of his proposal. Although he did cast a wistful glance back to the kitchen. He really could have done with a refill of coffee.

"You don't handle change very well, do you my darling?" he murmured, following his words with a kiss that was more a gentle brushing of lips.

Arrested by his comment, Thea frowned up at him, turning it over in her mind.

"It's not change so much, it's …"

Her voice trailed away as she sought the right words to make him understand.

"It's … I think, …" It wasn't like her to be so indecisive.

Finally discovering the words to explain herself, she gabbled them out before she lost her courage.

"It's giving someone else power over me. Over my heart. It scares the life out of me to feel so vulnerable. Marriage is pretty much the ultimate in handing over power, isn't it?"

"It can be." Josh picked his way carefully through the minefield which had opened up at his feet. "But Thea, it doesn't have to be. If the love is reciprocated, so is the sharing of power over each other. My vision of marriage is a sharing relationship. I see no need to try to change you, or dominate you. I love you as you are. We'll undoubtedly argue sometimes – this morning for example – but I'll always listen to your opinion and respect your decisions."

He followed his words with another kiss. One that left them both gasping and trembling in each other's arms.

"I'll hold you to that promise," Thea whispered.

Which required more kisses to seal the deal.

"Do you need to open the salon?"

Josh drew back, hoping the answer to this question was 'No'. It wasn't. Thea took her business seriously and would never leave her clients or staff in the lurch. She wriggled off his lap, leaning down to lay a final kiss on his lips.

"Can I just ask one question, Love?" Josh kept a hold of her hand as she made to step away. Thea nodded.

"Don't take this the wrong way, will you? What made you change your mind so quickly? Last night I was sure you'd refuse me. Hence the Jameson's."

"I didn't want to, but accepting seemed way to scary." Feeling more comfortable now, Thea prepared to open up.

Josh had been honest with her. She needed to reciprocate. Wanted to.

"When saying 'Yes' seemed too full of pitfalls, I asked myself how I'd feel if I said 'No'." She almost told him about her midnight phonecall to Eddie, only had the feeling that might be too much information. *Keep it simple,* she ordered herself.

"Imagining saying 'No' to you was so awful I couldn't bear to think about it. I knew I'd regret it for the rest of my life if I did." She gave him a wavering smile which grew in radiance as she remembered the euphoria she'd felt, making an affirmative decision.

"I really do love you, Josh Marten. Enough to take a chance on you. I am very happy to accept your proposal of marriage."

The salon opened at nine on the dot, but its proprietor had to beg her staff to hold the fort long enough for her to have a quick shower and dress before making an appearance. Angie Morgan, her first appointment of the day received a discount voucher to compensate her for having to wait long enough to flick through two magazines.

Next door, Josh Marten whistled as he stacked the dishwasher and cleaned the kitchen.

Epilogue

"I don't know why you have to be in such a rush, Thea," Dot grumbled as they neared Tamworth. "It takes time to find the perfect dress then have it hemmed and altered to fit. Four weeks is barely long enough. You're as bad as your sister."

In the front seat of Sophie's new Subaru Forester, the sisters exchanged unrepentant grins.

"We're in love, Mum. We can't wait to be together. It's really not that hard to pull a wedding together," Thea cheerfully answered, turning in her seat to smile at her mother. Going on, she proceeded to tick off the checklist on her fingers.

"The church is booked. The club for the reception; and the invitations went in the mail last night. Eddie says she'll have flowers for us, and I've spoken to Marge about accommodation for the guests. My friend Caterina is doing the photos, so it's just the dresses for the three of us left, then we're done. With time to spare."

Sophie, remembering her own hastily organised wedding, laughed at the expression on her mother's face.

"And *you* don't have an election day clashing with your wedding, Thea. Easy-peasy."

Not so easy-peasy four hours later when, standing outside the last wedding boutique in Tamworth, Thea's shoulders slumped defeatedly.

"God, Thea. You're so damn fussy. At least six you declared 'all wrong' looked absolutely perfect on you," complained Sophie, only adding to her misery.

"Well girls," ever the peacemaker, Dot sought to ward off an argument between her daughters. "On the plus side, Sophie. You and I have our dresses. Now, if you girls don't mind, I'm parched. And my feet are killing me." She shifted uncomfortably from foot to foot.

"Then I think the next stop better be a really nice cafe."

On the way back to the car after their late lunch, Dot and Sophie were chatting about the things Sophie still had to do at her house before returning to Canberra in two days time.

Tossing a question over her shoulder to Thea who'd been trailing along behind them, she halted, her hand on her mother's arm, bringing her to a halt beside her.

"We've lost Thea. Better back-track and find her. I don't think she knows her way around Tamworth very well yet."

They didn't have far to go. Back round the last corner they'd turned they found their quarry standing spell-bound in front of a shop window.

"Hey, Thea. What have you found?" Sophie called breaking the spell.

Thea turned, her face lit up in excitement.

"I've found it. Look! It's exactly what I've been looking for." Her voice softened on the last words and a mushy, rapt expression settled on her expressive face.

Exchanging speaking looks and raised brows, the other two women hurried up to her. They'd been a bit worried over her at lunch. She'd seemed so sunk in despondency. They found her staring at an Edwardian wedding gown, complete with picture hat covered in artificial flowers and a parasol.

"Isn't it lovely?" Voice hushed and dreamy, Thea turned back to the outfit on the mannequin.

"Yes. But …"

Dot, fearing to offend this new daughter she didn't really know all that well, allowed her instinctive protest to trail off into nothing.

Sophie wasn't nearly so careful.

"It's pretty, I suppose, but it's just an old bit of tat. This is an op-shop, Thea, in case you haven't noticed."

Snapping out of her introspection, Thea opened her mouth to refute her sister's dismissal of her find, then changed her mind.

"I'm going to try it on," she announced, pushing the door open and entering the shop.

Exchanging another look, this one with rolled eyes – Sophie's – Dot and Sophie followed in her wake.

"I'm not sure exactly what size it is, as it was hand-made," the shop assistant was saying, "but it might fit. Only one way to find out."

With that, she began carefully removing it from the model with Thea's eager assistance. Watching helplessly, Dot and Sophie were left holding the hat and parasol while several volunteer workers scurried in from the back room to join the show.

"We only put it in the window a few minutes ago," one said.

"It's special. I knew it'd find someone," another commented while they waited for Thea to emerge from the change-room.

"It fits." Dot's voice was tinged with disappointment when Thea emerged.

"Like a glove." Thea did an excited little twirl to show of the dress.

"Pity it's gone yellow with age. You'll never get it white again. If you like it so much, why not buy it to wear as a stage costume. I'll bet Eddie is already planning a concert for next year."

"That's a good idea, Soph," Dot chimed in, supporting her younger daughter. "If this is the style you're looking for, I remember seeing a similar dress this morning, only you didn't even consider it, Thea dear."

She almost added, that if Thea had, she'd have saved them from traipsing all over town for hours, but, still being careful, chose not to.

Ignoring all the comments, Thea pirouetted slowly in front of the cheval glass, studying her reflection from every angle.

"Pass me the hat," she said, not taking her eyes off the glass. The shop assistant hurriedly took it from Dot's limp grasp and reverently positioned it on Thea's head at exactly the right angle.

"Ooh," breathed one of the other women. "You look just like Audrey Hepburn in *My Fair Lady*."

"What do you think?" Thea turned to face her audience, which had swollen to include a couple of regular customers who'd wandered into the shop in search of interesting bargains.

"Looks made for you, Luv," one of them said. Everyone except Dot and Sophie nodded their agreement.

"But it's so yellowed," Dot protested feebly.

Thea fingered the silk and lace thoughtfully, then came to a decision.

"You've both chosen gold-toned dresses, so a bit of yellowing won't matter. It just feels so lovely on. As if it's had a happy history. It spoke to me as soon as I saw it." She turned to the shop assistant at her side.

"I'll take it."

The glow on her face silenced her family's protests. It was Thea's wedding, after all, and if this old relic was her choice …

"We'll stop by the dry cleaners and see what they can do to freshen it up," Dot offered, accepting the inevitable with a good grace.

Sophie, scrutinising the accessories, followed her mother's example.

"If we remove these tired old artificial flowers, Eddie could replace them with live blooms. I noticed her crepuscular rose is in bud. Being a creamy yellow, it'll be a perfect match."

Thea's answer was to hug them both.

~~~~~

On the day, Josh, his brother at his side, stared spell-bound at his beautiful bride, who, equally spellbound, couldn't take her eyes off him as she progressed slowly down the aisle.

Taking her place at Josh's side when Rob, her brother-in-law, handed her over to Josh's care, their love for each other shone so brightly there was a collective "Aah," from the congregation.

Reverend Charles gave them a moment, then, with an indulgent smile, brought them back to the very important business at hand.

Dot on one side of the aisle, and Josh's mother on the other, wielded handkerchiefs throughout, both so happy for their children they couldn't stem the flow of their tears. As Dot said, when her friend Barbara Morgan laughed at her,

"It takes showers to make rainbows."

"Then there'll be no shortage of rainbows for these two," her other friend, Eddie, herself moist-eyed, murmured from her other side. "Or flowers either."

THE END

_____

I hope you enjoyed *Redeeming Josh Marten*

Please turn the page for a preview of Lena West's new Oxley Crossing Romance, *The Making of Joey Lambert.*

Lena West

Here is Your Preview of

The Making of Joey Lambert

An Oxley Crossing Romance, Book 6 in the series

LENA WEST

1

"Stop! Jeni, stop!"

Joey Lambert swung round on hearing the shouting to see a little girl dashing after a soccer ball rolling out onto Bridge Street, the main highway through Oxley Crossing. Closer than the woman doing the shouting, he instinctively raced forward, grabbing a fistful of the girl's shirt a split second before she ran in front of a semi-trailer. The driver gave a blast on his horn, and a thumbs up to Joey as he roared by.

"My ball!" wailed the girl as she was hauled back onto the footpath and released.

"Jeni! You nearly got skittled by that truck. Your ball's not that important." Flinging herself to her knees, the slight, blonde woman clutched the girl, Jeni, tightly against her chest, looking gratefully up into Joey's eyes, her own brimming with tears. "Thank you, Mister." Her voice shook, and she took a breath before continuing. "Thank you so much. She mightn't realise how close an escape she had, but I do."

A brief, radiant smile bloomed as she stood, tilting her head to look up at her daughter's saviour.

A man head and shoulders taller than her meagre one hundred and fifty-seven centimetres.

"My pleasure, Ma'am." Joey blushed to the roots of his mop of overlong carroty curls, even his freckles taking on a rosy glow.

He'd noticed this pretty young woman several times since the New Year long weekend. Often enough to conclude she must have taken up residence in The Crossing, since casual visitors never stayed longer than a day or two at a time.

Often enough to begin scheming how to get up close and personal. Her child at her side had been all that held him back from approaching her. Married women were totally off limits to his way of thinking. He ran his hand through his hair, then, dusting it off on his jeans, offered it to her.

"Couldn't just stand there and watch her get hit. Joey Lambert, Ma'am. Glad I could be of service."

The blue eyes dropped away from his, as if the cracks in the pavement were more interesting. Straight white teeth bit her bottom lip, as the young woman hesitated briefly before taking Joey's hand, making him wonder indignantly if she thought the contact would contaminate her.

As she shook hands, she flashed a quick upward glance, smiling politely with none of the radiance of her first smile.

"Nikita Smith. Nikki. Pleased to meet you Joey. And this is my daughter, Jeni Smith." She gave the girl a gentle nudge to remind her of her manners.

"Thank you for saving me, Mr Lambert."

"You've got pretty names, you and your Mum." Self-conscious with hero status, Joey sought to change the subject.

"Do you think so? Grandma says when your name is Smith, you need something a bit different to 'stinguish it from all the other Smiths."

"Is that what your Daddy says, too?" Joey laughed, attempting to turn his blatant curiosity into a joke; surprised when the outgoing child turned shy.

"I don't have a daddy," she mumbled.

Embarrassment turned Joey's face redder than his hair.

"Sorry." He looked at the child's mother, repeating his apology. "Sorry, Mrs Smith. Foot-in-mouth is one of my many failings."

Beneath his embarrassment, renewed hope flared in his breast thinking this woman, the most appealing he'd seen in quite a while, might be available after all.

"Do you live here in Oxley Crossing, Jeni?" Questioning the child was a risk that had Joey holding his breath. Especially on top of his previous gaffe.

Out of the corner of his eye, he saw Nikki Smith frown at her daughter; but when she made no move to put a stop to the conversation, he breathed a little easier.

"Yes, Mr Lambert." Jeni was once again as free with her smiles as Nikki was parsimonious. "Mummy's a teacher," she added, pride shining bright in every ounce of her being. "She's going to start work as soon as the holidays are over."

Joey's heart sank again. 'Teacher' meant a university education. He'd flirted unsuccessfully with other young teachers a time or two.

He did an honest day's work for an honest day's pay, and found it offensive when a pretty girl talked down to him as if a mere yard hand at the sawmill was beneath her. As if his lack of education meant he lacked intelligence. With a pack of younger siblings his parents couldn't afford to send him to uni, and he'd taken the best job he could get in The Crossing.

But, ever the optimist, he thought maybe this girl was different. Maybe she'd realise he wasn't stupid. He'd see.

"Mummy, can I go and get my ball, now? I can see it in the gutter across the road." Jeni interrupted his musings.

"I'll get it," Joey volunteered, then, returning a moment later, ball in hand, he pushed his luck a little further.

"How about joining me for a coffee at Tan's?" He gestured to the bakery-café beside them.

This time it was Nikki, eyes cast down to the pavement again, who blushed.

Shy? Joey's eyes opened wide. He hadn't realised shy girls still existed. He was used to them being as assertive as the blokes. His pulse rate accelerated slightly.

"I'd like to Joey. I really would."

Nikki flashed him another of those split-second smiles, then lowered her eyes again.

"I've got an appointment to get my hair trimmed. I'll be late if I don't get going."

"Say hello to Thea and the girls for me," Joey said. Then, optimist to the last, asked, "Can we take a raincheck on the coffee?"

"That would be good. Bye Joey, and thanks again for saving my girl." She gave a little wave and, taking Jeni's hand, quickly disappeared round the corner.

"Bye Mr Lambert," Jeni called. "Thanks for bringing my ball back."

Joey stood staring after them for a moment, then giving himself a mental shake, headed off in the opposite direction, back to the tiny flat he rented behind Bill Whitman's place. He'd pulled a swifty there, beating out a couple of other blokes looking for accommodation. The idea of continuing to share the sleepout at the farm with his younger brothers had been incentive enough to urge him to approach Hazel Whitman as soon as Robert won the election and moved to Canberra, vacating the flat behind his parents' house.

Whistling as he walked, he pulled up short in front of the library. Nodding to himself, he pushed open the door and strolled in.

"Hi Aunt Eddie," he called, following the greeting up with a smacking kiss on the lips. Edith Patterson, the librarian, blushed and tittered.

"You and your nonsense, Joey Lambert," she bridled. "How can I help you?"

"With what you're best at, Eddie. Advice and information. With all the layoffs recently, I've been thinking it'd be a wise move to look for another job. Maybe acquire a few decent qualifications along the way."

"Wonderful, Joey. I told you years ago that's what you ought to do."

"You did. I listened, and here I am Aunt Eddie."

She wasn't really his aunt, but she'd taken him under her wing a long time ago when he'd been the victim of the school bully, and ever since she'd been his honorary aunt.

"Then let's go into my office and discuss your options over a coffee. Gail," she called to her assistant, "hold the fort for me, Dear."

Lena West

To get

"The Making of Joey Lambert"

as soon as it's released.

Go to

www.lenawestauthor.com

and make sure that you are signed up for news and release notices!

About the Author

Born in tropical North Queensland, Lena loves living close to the sea, although she moved frequently during her early years, living everywhere from Capital cities to isolated farms. Her most recent home has a deck overlooking the sea, which is her favourite room in the house, although, when the local birds come to visit, it is often hard to retreat to the computer and write!

After working as a primary school teacher in both her native Queensland, and later in New South Wales where she met her own romantic hero, she took a very early retirement to travel Australia with him, in a motorhome. This idyllic lifestyle lasted several years, during which she took the first steps towards fulfilling her lifelong ambition to write.

Storytelling came naturally - she had been making up stories for her own entertainment all her life, but it wasn't until she began traveling that she had time to write down some of her favourites. Now a self-published author, *Marrying Alan Morgan*, is the first in a series of rural romances set in the fictional town of Oxley Crossing. She also writes standalone contemporary romances and Australian historical romances.

With an addiction to happily-ever-afters, in both her reading and her own stories, the romance genre was a natural fit, and the variety of places she has lived have all added to the settings in which she brings love to life.

You can find Lena on Facebook at:

https://www.facebook.com/LenaWestAuthor/

or sign up for her newsletter at:

www.lenawestauthor.com

Other Books by Lena West

Historical Romances

Unto Death

https://www.amazon.com/dp/B07D3MZ1L4

Emily's Baby (Coming soon)

Lena West

Standalone Contemporary Romances

Loving Fenella

https://www.amazon.com/dp/B07B3RLS98/

Contemporary Series

The Wylde Flower Series

Book 1: Acacia's Story - FORGOTTEN (Coming soon)

Love in Oxley Crossing Series

Marrying Alan Morgan

https://www.amazon.com/dp/B0774V1L25/

Saving Jonathon Armitage

https://www.amazon.com/dp/B0788GCQJQ

Finding Mr Wright

https://www.amazon.com/dp/B07C98B7PJ

Electing Robert Whitman

https://www.amazon.com/dp/B07KWKLJG6

Lena West

Redeeming Josh Marten

The Making of Joey Lambert (Coming soon)

Connect with Lena!

Be the first to know about it when Lena's next book is released!

Sign up to Lena's newsletter at

www.lenawestauthor.com